A BAD ÉCLAIR DAY

BOOK 4 OF THE STRANDED IN PROVENCE MYSTERIES

SUSAN KIERNAN-LEWIS

SAN MARCO PRESS

A Bad Éclair Day. Book 4 of the Stranded Provence Mysteries.

Copyright © 2017 by Susan Kiernan-Lewis.

All rights reserved.

A Bad Éclair Day. Book 4 of the Stranded Provence Mysteries. Copyright © 2017 by Susan Kiernan-Lewis. All rights reserved.

Life in post-apocalyptic France has finally begun to settle down.

The cafés all have candles, the bakery ovens are all coal-fired and reliance on electricity and electronics are now a thing of the past. So when the Provençal village of Chabanel decides to go ahead with its annual pastry contest, it's a shock to everyone when one of the celebrity judges down from Paris dies a gruesome—and very public—death.

When a plate of poisoned chocolate éclairs turns out to be the murder weapon, it's up to expat and amateur sleuth Jules Hooker to prove that the little old ladies who made them aren't the murderers.

Because much in the same way that Jules can't stop after one *profiterole*, it soon becomes clear that this murderer doesn't intend to stop with one dead chef.

∽

Books by Susan Kiernan-Lewis

The Maggie Newberry Mysteries

Murder in the South of France
Murder à la Carte
Murder in Provence
Murder in Paris
Murder in Aix
Murder in Nice
Murder in the Latin Quarter
Murder in the Abbey
Murder in the Bistro
Murder in Cannes
Murder in Grenoble
Murder in the Vineyard
Murder in Arles
Murder in Marseille
Murder in St-Rémy
Murder à la Mode
Murder in Avignon
Murder in the Lavender
Murder in Mont St-Michel
Murder in the Village
Murder in St-Tropez
Murder in Grasse
Murder in Monaco
Murder in the Villa
Murder in Montmartre
Murder in Toulouse
A Provençal Christmas: A Short Story
A Thanksgiving in Provence
Laurent's Kitchen

The Claire Baskerville Mysteries

Déjà Dead
Death by Cliché
Dying to be French
Ménage à Murder
Killing it in Paris
Murder Flambé
Deadly Faux Pas
Toujours Dead
Murder in the Christmas Market
Deadly Adieu
Murdering Madeleine
Murder Carte Blanche
Death à la Drumstick
Murder Mon Amour
A Killable Feast

The Savannah Time Travel Mysteries
Killing Time in Georgia
Scarlett Must Die
The Cottonmouth Club
A Haunting on Forsyth Street
Savannah is Burning

The Stranded in Provence Mysteries
Parlez-Vous Murder?
Crime and Croissants
Accent on Murder
A Bad Éclair Day
Croak, Monsieur!
Death du Jour
Murder Très Gauche
Wined and Died
Murder, Voila!

A French Country Christmas
Fromage to Eternity
Crepe Expectations

The Irish End Games
Free Falling
Going Gone
Heading Home
Blind Sided
Rising Tides
Cold Comfort
Never Never
Wit's End
Dead On
White Out
Black Out
End Game

The Mia Kazmaroff Mysteries
Reckless
Shameless
Breathless
Heartless
Clueless
Ruthless

Ella Out of Time
Swept Away
Carried Away
Stolen Away

1

MAKING ENDS MEET

The farmer heaved his bulk over the split rail fence, grunting as he managed the maneuver. As gallant as a cavalier, he then turned and helped his lady crawl over the fence. From where I lay in the undergrowth in my Valentino Pop Butterfly skort I could tell by the way he looked over his shoulder that he wasn't entirely confident he was alone.

As well he shouldn't be.

Monsieur Gaillard, forty-two, married with six children, was in the midst of what the French call a tryst—time-honored and unobjectionable, unless you happen to be *Madame* Gaillard, in which case, French or not, and time-honored or not, you are royally screwed. And I don't mean in the manner in which Monsieur Gaillard was presently anticipating.

I glanced overhead at the gathering rain clouds. It was bad enough to lay on the ground on a *sunny* day but I draw the line at mud. I knew I didn't need to actually see the two lovebirds *in flagrante* in order to get paid. Like most sensible wives, Madame Gaillard put a lot of stock on intent.

And from where I was sitting, Monsieur's Gaillard's intent was pretty clear.

Even so, I did need to capture the moment, so to speak. I steadied the old Agfa camera that my friend Thibault had given me and snapped off several pictures. I caught Gaillard holding his paramour's hand, his face stretched in a lascivious grin—honestly no sane person would interpret it as anything else—and I snapped him grabbing her bottom with both hands and pulling her to his chest where the coquettish thing wrapped her thick legs around his waist. Did I mention Madame Fabre is fifty if she's a day?

Oh, yeah. I just got my payday. *Click click click.*

It was probably the sound of the damn shutter clicking that alerted the two canoodlers to my presence. But I kept shooting. Guilty looks would work too.

"*Qui est là?*" Gaillard hollered over his lady love's broad back.

I stood up and took the final three shots of them ensnarled in each other's limbs. Madame Fabre shrieked as Gaillard unceremoniously dumped her on her only only-moments-before-coveted buttocks and reached for a rock on the ground.

I swiveled on one foot, the camera swinging around my neck on its strap, and bolted down the hill to the main road. I hunched my neck to try to make myself smaller, cursing Thibault's noisy camera as the flung rock whizzed by my face, missing me by inches. Or, I guess since we're in France, centimeters.

More rocks would be coming—assuming Gaillard didn't have a gun on him. I was pretty sure he didn't. Most French farmers had shotguns but by and large left them at home when they set out to *shtup* their mistresses in the surrounding fields.

I'd learned a lot in the few months since I'd turned American-private-eye-trapped-in-a-foreign- country.

And first and foremost was the necessity of having a clean escape route mapped out ahead of time so I didn't get shot, have a dog sicced on me, or get nailed in the back of the head with a rock.

All hazards of my new trade.

I could still hear Gaillard shouting but I had a good lead and the bike I'd parked in the ditch by the road was already in sight. Unless he was way faster than he looked, I'd make it with time to spare.

Regardless, my heart was pounding with terror. All it took was one wrong step in a pasture full of potholes to end up face down in the dirt with an irate two hundred and fifty pound man's foot on my back.

I heard the sound of another rock hitting the ground a few yards behind me which gave me a vague flash of relief. He was too far behind to hit me now. As long as I didn't trip...as long as I stayed on my feet...as long as I made it to my bicycle before Monsieur Jumbotron caught up ...I'd be fine.

Ever notice how the worst thing you can think of always happens as soon as you think of it?

2

AMERICAN PIE

In the end it turned out I had to walk my bike home since I was in no condition to ride it.

I suppose it could have been worse. In the brief moments before the fornicating farmer caught up with me I had enough time to envision in detail what that might look like.

When my foot hit that divot, I swear my life flashed before my eyes just like they always say. Even before I hit the ground I knew I wasn't getting back up. I knew the bastard would be on me.

What I didn't know was what he felt comfortable *doing* to me when he caught me.

My ankle screamed in pain as I pushed up onto my knees, looking around for a weapon—anything—to defend myself with. There was nothing.

He came at me like a raging bull—frothing at the mouth, his eyes wild with fury.

He wasted no time in ripping the camera from my neck which nearly took off one of my ears. I have to tell you it made me intensely grateful that I'd decided to wear studs that day and not hoops. He smashed the camera against a nearby boulder, the sound of it ricocheting up and down the quiet valley. Behind him I could see his portly ladylove coming huffing and puffing to watch the show.

This is post-apocalyptic France. I'm not saying there's not law and order any more but lines have been blurred and I happen to know for a fact that a lot of stuff goes on that doesn't get reported.

I struggled to my feet and as he turned from the destroyed camera to survey me—much as a cartoon wolf looks at a defenseless lamb—I pointed a finger at him.

"Now stop right there, Mister," I said in as commanding a voice as I could muster. "That is private property which... I am willing to forget about if you stop right now."

I knew the destruction of my camera would serve to do one of two things. Either its senseless and noisy demolition would sate Monsieur G's desire to rip me limb from limb or it would ratchet up his wrath. Whichever one it was, my only hope was to get ahead of it.

He took a step toward me—clearly indicating he was leaning toward the second mind set—when he stopped and looked askance at me.

"*Vous êtes l'Americaine?*" he asked in a deeply guttural voice.

"Yes, I certainly am," I said, not at all sure the admission wouldn't end up being much worse for me. "And as such I am protected by my American embassy and the full weight and auspices of the United States of America."

By this time Madame Fabre had arrived, red in the face and panting.

I'd been working hard on my French in the last couple of months and was able to make out their exchange as having to do with *why don't you beat the crap out of her, yes I would of course but she's the American* and *well, what difference does that make*, and *I've destroyed her camera she can do us no harm.*

Honestly, I could see the old hag was keen to have him lay into me—or maybe take a shot at me herself—but in the end she settled for a series of threatening glances and a final kick at the pieces of what was left of poor Thibault's camera.

The two of them cussed me out fairly energetically but allowed me to leave without any further damage.

By the time I'd limped back home to my farm two miles down the road my whole body was sore, I was still feeling the residual effects of having had the crap scared out of me, and my ankle hurt.

La Fleurette where I live is this giant ancient *mas* on the outskirts of the village of Chabanel. I live there with two old ladies—neither of whom speak English—two cats and a dog who once saved my life. For real.

The *mas* loomed into view from around the last curve in the road. It looked a little like an abandoned pile of rocks but the closer you got to it the more it began to resemble a very pleasing assembly of bricks and rocks.

A long winding unpaved driveway led to the front door and every window on the front of the house has a box crammed full of red geraniums.

As soon as I stepped across the threshold of the old farmhouse my adorable mixed-breed dog Cocoa scampered over to me. I could hear the old ladies Madame Cazaly and Madame Becque in the kitchen—can you believe they still make me call them *Madame*?—which is the largest room in the house. The floor is tile, the oven and cooktops prehistoric and the refrigerator—which no longer works of course—is used only to store pantry items. After greeting Cocoa, I

A Bad Éclair Day

crept up the slick stone steps to the second floor, careful not to let the ladies hear me enter.

Broken foot or not they would surely put me to work.

An hour later, after washing up and changing into sweatpants and matching top, I limped into the kitchen to find my elderly roommates—twin sisters and known in the village as *les soeurs*—bustling about the now extremely hot kitchen and making their famous chocolate éclairs.

Our friend Thibault Theroux is incredibly handy with making amazing gadgets and inventions out of bubble gum and string especially when you have no bubble gum or string. He created a large wood-fire oven for us shortly after the dirty bomb that went off over the Riviera created an electromagnetic pulse that took out all the electricity in France.

Frankly the oven is a beast to get hot and keep hot, and absolutely impossible to maintain any kind of specific *degree* of heat. But I'm constantly reminded by assorted helpful onlookers—and Luc DeBray, Chabanel's chief of police, used to be one of the most vocal—of the alternative, and so I put up with the smoke and the work and the splinters from jamming wood pieces into it because I still like a hot meal now and then. Ever since the microwave ovens and slow cookers became a thing of the past, it's this or nothing.

After I limped into the kitchen I was swamped with a barrage of care and concern that rained down on me from both the Madame Twins for my obvious injury. Nah, I'm just joking. As soon as I hobbled into the room, Madame Cazaly turned on me and barked out something that sounded remarkably like *why weren't you here an hour ago?*

My understanding of French is improving although I find it's really only the twins I'm understanding better so maybe that's mostly me figuring out their body language, facial expressions and just knowing their personalities. But whereas before I usually got the gist of what they were saying, I'm now picking up words and more and more subtleties.

Ha! Like either of them was ever subtle a day in their lives.

This has been a very busy week for everyone because of the big village bakery contest coming up day after tomorrow. I'd heard of little else for a month and of course Chabanel wouldn't let a little thing like a dirty bomb exploding over the Mediterranean prevent them from having their annual fête.

The Madame Twins are both awesome bakers and I can personally attest to that fact but they are maniacally driven to win one award in particular this year—the top prize for the best chocolate éclair. As a result, our kitchen at *La Fleurette* has been churning out chocolate éclairs like a factory.

You'd think after all these years, they'd have the recipe down pat but no, they're always tweaking and improving it. I can attest to that since I've eaten most of their attempts and half my clothes don't fit any more as a result.

Some people say the *choux* pastry is the most important part of the chocolate éclair. Others the filling. Still others, the glaze.

Me, I happen to know it's none of those. The most important part of the éclair is the oven and I know that because that is *my* particular responsibility in the whole sequence of things. It's my job to keep the wood cooker stoked and hot at a certain level because the milk, butter and sugar need to come to a boil. Letting the fire die down *even a little bit* so that it loses its boil and then has to reboil or worse, never comes to a boil, is as catastrophic, trust me, as the last world war—at least as far as *les soeurs* were concerned.

Like I said, my job—when I'm not out trying to catch wayward village spouses—was to watch the sweet milky concoction until it came to a boil, then remove the pan from the stove and immediately beat in the measured-out flour until the batter is completely smooth. Not just *mostly* smooth or even perfectly-as-far-as-Jules-was-concerned smooth but completely effing smooth.

Then back on the stove the batter goes with me shoving sticks and branches into the fire chamber to bring the heat up to about medium. Have you ever imagined how you make a stove *medium* heat when you don't have a dial to twist? How do the old ladies know? I mean, they've been using a modern stove for the last fifty years but somehow they can just eyeball the fire and know it's too hot or not hot enough.

Anyway, there's a certain thing the batter does which will alert you to whether or not it's achieved the next stage of development. You beat the batter until the mixture comes away from the edge of the pan! Have you ever even heard of such a thing? Me neither. But trust me, it does.

But are we done yet? Not on your life. I now firmly believe every single person who ever indulged in one mouthful of a chocolate éclair needs to know exactly what a pain in the ass it is to make. You'll enjoy that mouthful more. Or swear off eating one ever again. One or the other.

"Jules! *Prends la pâte à choux!*"

I came into the kitchen just in time to snatch the pan off the stove, careful to use the oven mitt that Madame Becque was shoving at me. Once I did I found the bowl of eggs and began to drop in the required number one by one, beating carefully after each addition.

La pâte à choux or *choux* for short, is a sort of eggy pastry and so the eggs are important. But if you've ever dropped an egg into a hot pan you know how quickly eggs will scramble on contact with heat and that is *not* something you want to risk with *choux*. Not unless you're okay with two little old ladies having twin heart attacks and carrying on like you just commended the Nazis for getting the trains to run on time.

I've learned the hard way that these two have zero sense of humor about the war or baking. And not necessarily in that order.

Thank goodness once I'm able to incorporate all the eggs without it looking like egg drop soup, the sisters take over. They stuff the batter into a large piping bag and allow me to go about my business—which of course is inevitably *their* business since if I'm not out trying to prove some farmer's marital indiscretion, I am running errands for *les soeurs*.

Today, however, after making the *choux* batter, I'm looking forward to fifteen minutes with my left foot elevated. Just as I grabbed the cooling shell of a baked éclair and limped toward the living room, Cocoa began barking and ran toward the front door.

"Jules, *la porte!*" Madame B called out.

I took two quick bites of the pastry shell and hobbled to the door. *Naturally you'd want the crippled person in your group to be your doorman*, I grumbled to myself as I opened the door.

3

HOME FIRES

"Jules!" Katrine Pelletier flung out her arms and embraced me while her two little girls ran past me to find Cocoa who was wisely backtracking into the house at warp speed.

Katrine was my first friend in Chabanel—if you don't count the girl in my first apartment who eventually tried to murder me. Katrine had been through a lot recently with the dramatic break-up with her husband—who likewise tried to murder me. Huh. I think I'm seeing a pattern here.

"You don't mind?" Katrine said, her cheeks flushed from the chill in the late afternoon air. "*Les soeurs* said they would give Annette and Babette a cooking lesson today."

"Are you kidding? I'm thrilled. It's been ages since we talked." I ushered her into the living room while Madame B came to corral the little girls, ages eight and nine, away from poor Cocoa and into the kitchen. When I saw Madame B's eyes light up at the sight of the little girls it reminded me that, having never married, she had no grandchildren of her own.

I knew the Madame Twins would fuss at me if I didn't

offer Katrine a drink but before I could lurch off into the kitchen to find something, Madame C showed up with a tray of two coffees in little demitasse cups.

Katrine thanked her warmly but I was flabbergasted. In spite of what Madame C would have me believe, it meant she'd noted I was hurt. She refused to get eye contact with me so I murmured my thanks and watched her return to the kitchen.

Léa Cazaly was an interesting old girl and I'm sure however long I'm privileged to know her I'll never get to the bottom of who she is or what makes her tick.

"So, *chérie*?" Katrine said settling into the couch with her coffee. "How is work?"

I flashed back to the memory of Monsieur Gaillard towering over me and the conviction I'd had that he was about to pummel me and my favorite Stella McCartney denim vest into the French dirt.

"I'm rethinking my career options," I said. "Any openings in the cheese business?"

Katrine had a small herd of goats and she and her mother made *chèvre* that Katrine sold at the local market. When I first met her she was making a decent living. At the time she was convinced people would continue to pay her in money and that the money would continue to hold value. In the months since the EMP I wasn't sure if that was still true. Losing her husband hadn't helped and I know life had gotten way harder for her.

She smiled tiredly. "I could use the help, *bien sûr*," she said. "But I could not pay you."

"Story of my life," I said with a sigh.

"Let us talk of happier things. How is your sex life being?"

"It is being fine, thanks," I said a tad defensively. I knew she was going to bug me about giving Luc DeBray the heave-ho last month. The Madame Twins practically made it their daily mantra to harangue me about that.

"Have you seen Luc recently?"

"You know I haven't and you know why I haven't," I said. It was vastly annoying to me that nobody seemed to credit me with the reason *why* I stopped seeing Luc.

Correction. We hadn't really been *seeing* each other to start with. It had looked like we were about to when Luc blocked an opportunity for me to return to the States.

Isn't that a decent enough reason not to want to date someone? Because they willingly—deliberately—stopped you from going back to your own country? Am I right?

Well, apparently I was the only one in Chabanel who thought so. At least in my inner circle.

But maybe that's because they weren't there for the moment six weeks ago when it all came crashing down around us. I remember vividly the image of Luc standing on my back patio, his anger crackling around him like a living thing:

"Clearly I can do nothing about you endangering yourself here in the village," Luc said. *"Jumping into cars of murderers or breaking into bakeries at night where murderers sleep—but as for the things I can control, I will."*

"You would prevent me from returning to my own country? You can't do that!"

"I can if I think it's too dangerous."

"I have the right to do something dangerous! I have free will!"

"No, you don't. Not where it comes to your safety."

"I detest you!"

"I can live with that. But you're not leaving. Once the airlines are running again, fine. Fly away home as fast as you can."

"I will! And I can't wait!"

"Bon. When that times comes I will drive you to the airport myself."

That moment was six weeks ago on a lovely evening when we should have been celebrating. When Luc and I were done shouting at each other, he left *La Fleurette* and we'd not exchanged another word since.

"Is it true you're dating Jim Anderson?" Katrine said with an arched eyebrow. Boy, she was nearly as good as Madame C with that whole unspoken admonishment thing.

Jim Anderson was the only other American in the area and someone who'd been very supportive of me since the moment I landed in Provence.

Plus he was really, really cute.

"Jim and I are seeing each other, yes," I said. "Is that okay with you?"

Honestly, after that whack-job of a husband of hers I'm surprised Katrine had the nerve to try to give me advice on whom I should date. It's possible she could read my mind because she blushed and looked away and I felt instantly contrite.

I knew Katrine was in contact with her husband Gaultier and I knew she *said* it was because he was the girls' father but I also knew Gaultier had a hold over Katrine that neither of us would ever understand.

Men.

Am I right?

∼

Katrine's girls watched as Madame C wielded the piping bag and squeezed out twelve log-shaped squirts of pastry dough on a baking tray. In the old days—i.e. before the EMP last summer—the twins would then pop the baking tray in the freezer before baking. We don't have that option any more. Or well, we do but it's a major pain in the *derrière* to make it happen. The last town hall meeting, the mayor said we'd be getting limited electricity back in Chabanel so we were all excited about whenever that would happen.

I imagine in the US or Britain, having even limited electricity would be welcome for things like dialysis machines and hospital ventilators, but in France being able to freeze your *choux* before baking it was naturally considered at least as important.

You think I'm joking.

Hey, pastries are very important to these people. And if you could see how I'm straining at the seams of all the clothes I brought with me last summer, you'd see that they were clearly very important to me, too.

I definitely have to think about going on a diet but as Madame B has told me, laughingly, any time before the pastry festival was clearly not the time.

Anyway, so because we have to skip the freezing-the-batter step, Madame C pops the piped raw éclairs into the oven—with me steadily shoving chunks of wood in the hopper to keep the heat going.

You know, back in the day I never used to bake. Not even when all you had to do was rip open a box, give it a stir and toss the results in an electric oven. And yet here I am... sweating like a warthog on a chilly October day to keep the oven at just the right temperature so the extremely fragile puff éclairs don't burn or come out, God forbid, under done.

While I'm doing all this—and yes, I know to the

untrained ear it doesn't sound that complicated—Madame B is whipping up the chocolate custard that goes inside the tubes once they're out of the oven.

Katrine's little girls are watching all of it with eyes as big as dessert plates. I'm sure they remember what life was like before the EMP but they look too young to have been very involved with electronic toys or tablets.

Still, even little kids remember TV. And yet these girls don't seem to mind that there's been no cartoons for the last five months. They're watching *les soeurs* as avidly as if the two of them were Food Network's latest cooking show. Just the thought of it made me laugh but when I turned to roll my eyes at Katrine so we could both share in how ridiculously important everyone was treating this whole business, I saw that she was every bit as enthralled as her girls were.

Madame C swiftly tucked the tip of the custard bag into the end of one of the baked *éclairs* and a second later, she put it down and reached for another. I don't know what told her the *éclair* was sufficiently filled. I guess she'd just done it for so many years she knew by feel. Within moments all the éclairs were filled and Madame B stepped up with a ceramic bowl. She used a large serving spoon to drizzle chocolate glaze across the tops of all the éclairs. Normally, she'd then set the finished éclairs in our icebox to allow the glaze to set but with a barely imperceptible nod from Madame C—both girls and Katrine reached for their éclairs.

If you like *éclairs*—and honestly, what weirdo doesn't like chocolate éclairs?—you can imagine the groans of ecstasy and rapture that emitted from everyone in the room for the next several moments.

I know *les soeurs* were working on their recipe renditions for the upcoming contest, but if you could see the look of pride and delight on both their faces when those little girls wolfed down their éclairs, you'd know that making chocolate éclairs had nothing at all to do with blue ribbons or professional accolades.

∼

Agathe Zabala sifted the flour into the large bowl.

This batch of éclairs would be the one she would put up for judging. It would be the one that would take the top prize. Of that she was sure. After all, had her éclairs not won every year for the past three years?

This year would be no different.

She heard the door slam as Tristan let himself out and she felt a fissure of anger jolt through her. He had been here to ask for money again. Adele's boy.

She wiped a thin sheen of sweat from her upper lip and noticed her hands were trembling.

Today she could too easily see Tristan's great grandfather in him. In his sharp blond features, his cruel eyes. Even the hair lip, which the gypsies think is a person's sin made visible, was an admonishment aimed at her. She flushed with humiliation.

Damn him! Damn him for coming here!

Damn him for living!

This was Agathe's daughter Gigi's final insult—and the ones from the grave are always the worst. Hadn't Agathe paid for her crime over and over again, time and time again?

Tristan was only the most recent reproach for the crime everyone knew she owned.

She cracked two eggs into a bowl.

But the end was coming.

There was at least some peace in that.

4

MARKING TIME

Luc stared out his office window. He did that less and less these days. It was amazing how just walking through the village and seeing Jules with Jim Anderson could serve to ruin the rest of Luc's day.

It was his own fault. To let it get to him like that. Thankfully, he hadn't witnessed any signs of intimacy between the two but he knew they were together. He'd heard the gossip. What he hadn't been able to avoid was the pitying looks from Eloise along with the scornful smirks from his second in command, Adrien Matteo.

How the whole village had got it in their heads that Luc and Jules were once a couple or were destined to be a couple he had no idea.

It probably had something to do with the fact that until recently he'd spent almost every evening at *La Fleurette*.

Luc shook himself out of his thoughts, knowing he had little time for such self-indulgent reflection. Tomorrow's pastry fête would bring with it its own set of problems—as it always did.

"Are you even listening to me, Chief DeBray?" the mayor

said with exasperation. Lola Beaufait had been mayor of Chabanel for nearly twenty years, although in the right light she still looked as if she'd just stepped off the fashion runway of Paris where she'd spent the first part of her career.

A village girl who'd abandoned the village as soon as she was old enough—and some might say fourteen was plenty old enough, especially if you looked like Mademoiselle Beaufait—Lola returned home after making her name, her fortune and her fair share of shame and scandal in Paris and Milan to claim her role as the village mayor.

Luc turned to face the mayor. He and Lola had a symbiotic relationship in that they both loved their village but unfortunately had very different ways of how that might be manifested.

"Repeat that last bit," he said with an unapologetic shrug.

Lola's eyes snapped with annoyance.

"I said that it is very important that the visit from Chef Chevalier and his protégé come off without a hitch."

"And why would it not?"

Lola ignored his comment. "Chef Chevalier is a close personal friend of Madame Dinot. The right word in her ear could translate into untold advantages for Chabanel."

Madame Dinot, the wife of the current French president, was about the same age as Lola who Luc guessed to be in her mid-fifties. As much as Lola had trotted the globe in her day, he wondered if she knew the woman personally?

"Untold advantages such as?" He wasn't deliberately trying to be difficult but in his experience with Lola it didn't do to get ahead of her.

"Such as electricity?" Lola said with exasperation. She stood up and walked to the window edging him away. He detected the scent of Chanel 5. In many ways, this new world order of theirs was harder on Lola than anyone. To live without electricity? Cars? Trains or air travel?

Although like himself, Lola had access to basic communications via satellite phone, the technology was cumbersome and time-consuming.

Life nowadays must be a living hell for her.

"The Chabanel bakers are all using wood fires for their ovens," Luc said mildly, knowing that wasn't her point but needing her to get to it before his day was over.

She threw him a piercing glance as if wondering if he were being insubordinate. He looked blankly back ensuring that she had no ammunition to work with.

"And," he continued, "Chabanel should receive the reduced-capacity generators by the end of next month." This would allow electricity in the village for reduced hours —just like in Aix.

"There is more to life than working lights," Lola said cryptically.

"But they are still very useful."

She made a face and strode to his desk where she snatched up her purse.

"Just make sure there are no problems with the pastry fête tomorrow," she said acidly.

~

Enora couldn't help thinking as the bus trundled relentlessly through the bland ugly countryside of the last time she'd been to Provence.

She'd sworn she'd never return.

She glanced at the other pastry chef, Lucien Chevalier, who was reading in his seat. She wondered why she'd agreed to do this with him. Why Chabanel of all places. Why now?

But in her heart she knew. She had always known.

This was the end of the line. It was now and it was for good.

As hard as that had been to come to, it felt good for it to finally be arrived at.

Let the chips fall.

"You should see your face, *chérie*," Lucien said. "All scrunched up like you forgot the sugar in the *tarte citron*." He sneezed twice in quick succession and went back to his book, uninterested in whatever response she might have had to that.

Enora was used to that. After two years with him she was used to that and much more.

The restaurant he worked at had a Michelin star. She knew he'd be just as repulsive with or without the star. But it hadn't helped.

He sneezed again and Enora found herself annoyed by the fact that he would make this trip while sick with a cold.

That was Lucien. As usual.

With absolutely no care for anyone else he might infect along the way.

5

HALF BAKED

I'd say Katrine and her little lambs had been gone about an hour before I realized I was about to lose my mind. The energy and heat index had ramped up to nuclear levels in the kitchen but as I'm sure I've mentioned before any chance I might entertain of escaping the chaos was erased the moment Madame C saw me doing only two or three things at once and decided I'd had enough loafing around.

"Jules, go to the *boulangerie*," she said in French. "*Immediatement!*"

"Of course," I said indicating the groaning tables of the dozens and dozens of frosted éclairs, "because one thing we need right now is *more* pastries."

"Bread for tonight's dinner," Madame B said with a smile and an admonishing wag of her finger. *That silly Jules! Always trying to get out of work. Now take your broken ankle and hoof it the three miles into town and get us some bread!*

I knew better than to argue. If I tried, their remarkable and uncanny grasp of the English language would vanish as quickly as would any chance I ever had of not going to the bakery.

As soon as I turned toward the door and my jacket hanging on the wooden dowel next to it, I realized that a little fresh air and some time away when I wasn't stoking a fire, grabbing a pan of éclairs or finding myself elbow deep in dirty pots and clogged pastry bags wouldn't be such a bad thing.

"*Viens*, Cocoa!"

As soon as I called to her, the dog's ears perked up and she scampered over to me. I collected her leash but didn't bother connecting it. With no cars on the road and her dinner in the offing I had no worry about her running away. I shrugged into my denim jacket and began thinking of stopping into the Sucre Café for a quick *espresso*.

"Do not be long!" Madame C called out—as usual reading my mind in any language.

I've discovered October in the south of France isn't really cold. It's not at all balmy like Orlando or the Keys would be this time of year and once that pesky Mistral comes sidling in through the village streets, you'd think you were in Anchorage. But for the most part fall here is like the best part of a north Georgia fall—cool, crisp and sunny.

As I walked toward the village I actually felt my ankle feeling better. Huh. Maybe there really was something to the phrase *walk it off*? By the time I reached the first fork in the country road that led to Chabanel, I was walking without a limp.

Cocoa ran ahead of me sniffing at weeds on the side of the road. Once she darted into the long grass and disappeared but before I got to the first cobblestone street of the village, she was back by my side.

I'd had absolutely no experience with rural French

villages before I ended up stranded in one. So adjusting to how incredibly narrow the cobblestone roads were in Chabanel took me a while. And except for that first day when the taxi drove me here, I've never really seen it with actual vehicular traffic. I cannot imagine how cars ever managed to drive down these streets without regularly whacking off their side mirrors. Seems to me that the EMP was a good opportunity for France to go around widening all their medieval village roads. But hey, that's just me. I'm sure the French president has other ideas now that most of us aren't able to drive any more.

Fortunately for me and my now re-aching foot, the main village *boulangerie* is on the side of town that's closest to *La Fleurette*. It was already five o'clock so I knew the bakery would be jam packed with everyone in town trying to get their dinner bread. I hoped I wasn't too late and there would be something left. The Madame Twins were remarkably unforgiving about situations I had no control over but was just near enough to blame.

As I approached the bakery I connected Cocoa's leash and tied her up outside in case she decided to go home with someone coming out of the bakery who had food. I know she was devoted to me and she did save my life but hey, fresh croissants? Much like me, she wasn't so good at that whole delayed gratification thing.

Inside the *boulangerie* there were six people queuing up to the counter but I spotted a good half dozen baguettes in the racks behind where the proprietor was standing at the counter so I wasn't worried. If the baguettes sold out before I got there, I could see plenty of *boules* and *fougasse*—either of which would appease *les soeurs*.

The aroma inside any French bakery is one any normal person will take to her grave as one of life's top most exquisite experiences and that goes double when it's cold outside. You can practically *see* the sugar and the vanilla wafting in the air like floating stardust.

I've been in Chabanel nearly five months now and since it's a small village and I'm American everyone in town knows who I am. That's actually kind of cool in a lot of ways. Most people smile or talk to me on the street and it doesn't matter that I don't know who they are—or that my French is crap.

It was the same in the *boulangerie* too. The two women pressing up to the counter were too intent on getting just the right baguette for their dinners but everyone else in line was happy to turn around and greet me.

As I've mentioned my French still largely sucks so I do a lot of smiling and head nodding and *bonjouring* and usually that suffices. Often people will ask me about *les soeurs* because everyone knows them. They're legends in this village because of what they did as members of the French resistance during the war.

True, that was a couple of million years ago but in France, memories are long even if they're not *your* memories but your parents' or your grandparents'. The Sisters Cazaly are revered in this town for their bravery and their tragedy —much of which is still a mystery which of course makes it much more tragic.

"*Bonjour*, Madame Hooker," the proprietor sang out to me. I don't care how you say it, my name has about as much grace as a lodged kidney stone.

I find that most shop owners sing out *bonjour* when you enter their shops but it doesn't mean they're particularly jolly or even feeling good. It's just what they do.

Madame Fournier, for example, who owns and runs the bakery is about as sour as a woman can be. Surrounded by all this sugar and yeast? I know. I don't understand it either. Probably has to do with the fact that she's up at three every morning making bread and is forced to go to sleep every night while everyone else is out having *apèros* and listening to jazz and stuff.

"*Bonjour*, Madame Fournier," I say back to her with a big smile to show her how it's done. But she's already talking to someone else.

Just as I settle into my place in line there was a commotion at the front door. Two people—strangers to Chabanel—swept through the door and start to make a big deal about how cold it is outside which is so strange because I'm the biggest whinebag of all time and it was really only a little cool out.

The man was handsome. I saw that right off and I wasn't the only one who did. The woman next to me—I've seen her several times at the market on Wednesdays with her two small children—made a sexy kind of humming sound under her breath which made the other two women next to her cackle and nod in agreement.

The guy was wearing a cape for crap's sake so he was clearly into himself and that was underscored by the fact that he never got eye contact with a single one of us standing in line but simply strode ahead to the counter and rapped his gloved hand on the glass to get Madame Fournier's attention.

Now I don't know if you've spent any time in France but if you have you probably already know that the French don't always respect things like queues and personal space. But this! This was egregious! We were all standing in line, meek as can be, assuming our places in line would guarantee us the goods we'd come here to buy in a timely and fair fashion, and then here was this...this *stranger*...barging to the head of the line!

I was annoyed but hey, there was nobody behind me so him jumping the queue didn't put me out all that much but the woman who was next in line at the counter? And the one behind her? Trust me, you don't want to get between a French housewife and her dinner baton.

Witnessing what happened next from the back of the bakery was like seeing a mini-explosion—where you miss the actual detonation and all you see are the ripples in the airwaves of the explosion.

The screaming was immediate and it came from all sides. The woman who'd thought he was cute was now red in the face and jabbing her finger in his direction while the other ladies were actually reaching out to physically pull him back.

The cad had the nerve to slap away some of their hands as if they were annoying gnats not even worth his glance to see who was pawing at him. He spoke loudly to Madame Fournier and as he did his companion, a young woman with a short pixie haircut and thick eyebrows, came forward behind him. She put a hand on his back, but whether to support him or call him back, I couldn't tell.

As I said, my French is crapola but I'm beginning to pick up the basics as the weeks go by and let me tell you the basics that *Monsieur* jerk boy was laying on Madame Fournier were nearly as easy to translate as if I had subtitles.

First the guy sneered at her and threw his hands out to encompass all the baked goods in the glass case as if they were autopsy specimens. A few women gasped and one actually clapped a hand to her mouth in outright astonishment.

Madame Fournier stared at him, her face white, her lips

quivering as if she was trying to speak but no words came out.

The man coughed out a harsh laugh and then swung his hands out to indicate all of *us* with the same level of disdain and incredulity.

Hey, I may not understand all the words but even I know when I'm being dissed!

And as for the ladies standing in line? Well, they *did* know all the words and they were not happy about it.

"Lucien, *viens*," his companion said, her eyes raking Madame Fournier as coldly as if she were a piece of meat—and a rancid one at that. She said a bunch more and her words and her expression made it clear that she was saying something along the lines of *why waste your time on these ridiculous people?*

At least that's what *I* picked up.

In any case, the guy laughed again, turned and draped his arm around the girl's shoulder and the two of them pushed their way out of the crowd. There was something about the way they walked out together that I couldn't put my finger on. Lovers maybe? Not quite. But something definitely odd.

I couldn't see the young woman's face from where I was standing but the guy was laughing in a mean haughty way. Once he was gone, I turned to see Madame Fournier watching after him, her eyes big and full of tears. Then she abruptly turned and dashed into the back room leaving a room full of customers.

Since it didn't look like anyone was going to get any bread any time soon, I slipped out of the *boulangerie* to see which way the two strangers had headed.

They hadn't gone far. They both stood in the middle of the street in front of the shop. A young man was standing there too. I'd seen him before—he was hard to forget. He had white blond hair, sharp features and cold blue eyes.

But the most distinguishing thing about him, unfortunately, was the hair lip that twisted his mouth into a grimace that bared his bottom row of crooked teeth. I'd only seen him once before but I knew this was Madame Zabala's grandson Tristan.

I'd missed the moment when the three of them stopped to talk for whatever reason but what I didn't miss was the moment the stranger pointed at poor Tristan's face and laughed!

It is seriously unbelievable to me how cruel some people can be. I can sometimes understand when they're just being thoughtless lunkheads but what this man was doing was deliberate and calculated.

Tristan blushed scarlet which made his blond hair look bone white. His face was clenched in fury and frustration and he stood there, holding a thick walking stick in both hands until the man and the woman had moved on down the road, the man's laughter ringing in the air.

My first instinct was to tell Tristan he shouldn't pay that jerk any mind at all. My head ran through a few platitudes I might say to him about beauty being skin deep and stuff which in retrospect I'm immensely grateful I didn't get a chance to say. Not that Tristan would have understood them anyway. As it was, when he moved toward the sidewalk, I got eye contact with him and gave him what I hoped he'd interpret as a sympathetic look.

Yeah, um. No.

His face twisted into a visage of fury and shame. He lunged at me, snarling out, "*Visez votre pitié!*" Startled, I gave out an involuntary yelp. I honestly thought he was going to attack me. Unfortunately, Cocoa thought so too.

She lurched up from where she was tied to an ancient stone parking barricade between Tristan and me, the hair on her back bristling. She growled low and menacing.

I saw the next few seconds happen as if they were on a video being played back at half speed. I saw my dog—constrained by the leash so she'd never reach him—charge Tristan as he began to pass and I saw Tristan start, and then swing his club into the air.

Aiming at Cocoa's head.

I don't remember moving but I hit Tristan solidly in the back with both hands knocking his aim off so that he ended up smashed his club into the cobblestones near Cocoa.

"What is the matter with you?" I shouted at him, the sound of blood pumping in my ears. "You can't just go bashing people's dogs, you lunatic!"

By now, the rest of the shoppers in the bakery had filed out of the shop and were staring at me and Tristan like we were the next new post-apocalyptic reality show.

I saw Tristan look at them—and then at me—and while I have no idea what he would have done if there hadn't been an audience, I do know that when he saw he wouldn't be able to murder me or my dog as befitted his escalated temper, he screamed like a maniac and threw his bat into the front display window of Madame Fournier's *boulangerie*.

6

TILTING AT WINDMILLS

On the morning of the big pastry fête Luc stood solemnly next to Agathe Zabala and stared at her grandson Tristan. The boy had been arrested for vandalism the night before and spent the night in jail.

"I have already spoken with Madame Fournier," Madame Zabala said. "I will pay for the damages."

Luc nodded. He would release Tristan into Madame Zabala's care until the boy could face the charges against him that Madame Fournier insisted on pressing. It was a small village and nothing good could come of the spite, but Marie Fournier was not known for her loving or generous nature.

Luc glanced over at Tristan. It was just as well. The boy looked like he hadn't had much experience with those sorts of virtues anyway.

And neither would he find them at the bosom of his maternal grandmother it seemed.

"You are a horrible creature and I should let you rot in

jail!" Madame Zabala said to Tristan, grabbing his arm and attempting to push him toward the door.

Tristan snatched his arm away and bolted out the door.

"You cannot control him, Madame Zabala," Luc said. "It might have been better to leave him with me."

"I would love to leave him with you permanently, Chief DeBray," Madame Zabala said. "He is here to ruin my life." She shook her head and angry tears gathered in her eyes. "But his mother...I cannot do it to her memory."

She turned and followed her grandson out into the sunlight.

Luc watched the two walk toward where the fair was being held and tried to put the pieces together of their relationship. The kid acted like he hated his grandmother—and the whole world for that matter—and Madame Zabala wasn't much better.

Something kept them connected though.

Something terrible.

～

I can only imagine what the Chabanel *pâtisserie* fête must have been like when people had working ovens and refrigerators. It must have been amazing. It must have been a thing of beauty to behold and worth traveling to for miles around.

The pastry festival was set up in the square where the daily market normally took place, and featured a full city block crammed with an endless array of the most beautiful pastries, breads, cakes and tarts I'd ever seen.

While basically an opportunity for neighbors to show off their baking prowess and settle longstanding rivalries—although of course nothing ever got resolved—it was also a venue for craftsmen and artisans to sell their hand-made goods.

Being late fall, there was less produce and more crafts and woodworking items. The food truck that had operated in the village before the EMP was up and running once more although instead of ice cream and pizza, today it was serving *canelés* and *macarons*.

Kiosks, awnings, and tables formed the booths that would anchor the pastry contest—without argument the main purpose of the fête. Each of the village women who were participating had their own small booth. On one side of the booth they would sell samples of their hopefully award-winning baked goods, and on the other side was arranged a sampling of their most perfect specimens awaiting judgment by the chef judges.

As a result of the cool weather people were roasting chestnuts in dented and hopefully clean garbage can lids and selling cups of mulled wine. I've been to many festivals in the north Georgia mountains—complete with spicy, sweet barbecue and funnel cakes to die for, all crispy and hot and dusted with powder sugar—and I'm still going to have to weigh in on the side of the Chabanel pastry fête.

There really was a touch of magic in the autumn air.

If I'd only known then what this afternoon would bring, I'm sure it would have seemed a lot less enchanting.

The Madame Twins and I arrived early to arrange the chocolate éclairs so that they might be purchased on the broadest side of the wooden booth that one of the village men had helped us erect. Madame B laid out a hand-embroidered napkin on the shelf on the opposing side upon which she then placed a beautiful Spode platter arranged with what she and Madame C determined were their six best éclairs.

I have to say, the pastries looked beautiful, the drizzled chocolate on each one something Picasso himself would have wept to see. And I can personally attest to the fact that the actual *tasting* of these beauties was an explosion of perfection in your mouth that would never be replicated again in this lifetime.

Did I mention I wrote ad copy one summer after college?

As I watched all the activity in the fair, I have to admit I might have been looking for one person in particular. After all, the festival was a classic opportunity for pickpockets and the like so it stood to reason that Luc might be patrolling the area.

I saw Luc's second in command Adrien Matteo swaggering about the place. Naturally he stopped at every second food booth for free samples. It was no wonder he looked like a big BoBo doll stuffed in a police uniform.

I chided myself for being so ungenerous. It was true Matteo and I didn't get along—we'd despised each other at first sight—but I was working on trying to rein in my less than charitable thoughts.

Behind Matteo I spotted Jim Anderson, my erstwhile boyfriend, and I had to smile.

Jim was tall, with a big grin. He was smart too and unlike me, unfailingly generous to any and all. As I watched him make his way through the crowd I could see how people greeted him and I have to say if anything shows you the real measure of a person it's how the inhabitants of a provincial French village accept said person—a virtual stranger in their midst. Jim loved Chabanel and that counted for a lot to these people.

I waved and Jim grinned even wider and made his way over to me. Before he reached me I saw a minor commotion behind one of the contestant booths and realized it was the two celebrity chefs making their way through the crowd.

It was rather extraordinary, I thought, that they hadn't made an appearance at the festival before now—already a full hour into the festivities. I wasn't surprised to see that the two judges were none other than the two rude douchebags who'd reduced Madame Fournier to tears yesterday and caused Tristan to lose his cool to the tune of a very expensive bakery display window.

Jim kissed my cheek before turning to see what it was that was taking my attention.

Lucien Chevalier—Douchebag Number One—was walking past the food booths and reeling off a snickering commentary as he went by each one to the receptive giggles of the second chef—better known as Douchebag Number Two.

"What is their problem?" I said with exasperation. "Why did they agree to come and judge if they're just going to make fun of us?"

I have to admit, the thought that they would disparage the Madame Twins' éclairs after all the work and effort those two had put into them had smoke coming out of my ears.

"They're from Paris," Jim said with a shrug as if this was answer enough.

Behind the two judges Mayor Lola Beaufait was smiling and nodding—almost as if she were trying to undo all the enmity the two judges were causing.

At one point the male chef—Chevalier—pointed to a basket of croissants and made an acerbic comment to his companion which got the two of them laughing so much that Chevalier lapsed into a sneezing fit. Even Lola—as sycophantic as they come—was watching the display with a grimace of distaste. Not that she'd ever let the two guest judges see that. As soon as Chevalier turned to look at her, Lola's face was all smiles again.

It ain't easy being mayor.

As the two chefs and Lola made a slow—and I'm sure for Lola, increasingly agonizing—circuit around the festival of booths, I caught a glimpse of Madame Zabala pushing her way through the crowd.

Her booth was set up next to ours. Although *les soeurs* must have noticed that their arch enemy hadn't yet shown up—and was in fact an hour late—I knew they weren't worried.

That's because everyone in the village knew where Madame Zabala had been: bailing out that ragbag grandson of hers down at the *police municipale*. As soon as I saw Tristan trudging belligerently behind his grandmother, I realized that must be where Luc was—doing the paperwork for releasing Tristan into his grandmother's care.

Jim shook his head.

"Poor guy," he said. "He doesn't stand a chance in this town."

I looked at him in surprise. "You sound like you think he's getting a bad deal or something. Tristan makes his own problems. You did hear how he threw a huge stick into the window of the *boulangerie* yesterday, didn't you?"

"Of course. I also heard you were involved."

I felt a rush of indignation.

"If by *involved* you mean nearly attacked by that hoodlum, then yes I was involved."

"What happened exactly?" Jim said in an obvious ploy to mollify me.

"Half the village saw Tristan Zabala try to kill my dog

and then viciously destroyed Madame Fournier's display window."

"How did the cops know it was him?"

"You did hear the part where I said *half the village* saw it? One of them obviously reported it to the police."

He raised an eyebrow at me. This is something he must have picked up from the French. It's a body language that's extremely expressive if mildly indicting but there can be no mistake about the intent.

"Look," I said defensively. "I didn't stick around because there was no point. Everyone saw what happened and could describe what happened in much better French than I could."

When he still looked at me with a smile but mild disapproval, I said indignantly,

"Hey, I wasn't the one who broke the window."

"No, you just caused it to get broken."

"You can't be serious! If anybody *caused* it that would be that judge over there who stopped Tristan in the street to have a good laugh at the expense of his hair lip."

"Are you serious?" Jim looked in Chevalier's direction. "Who does that guy think he is?"

"I was just trying to offer Tristan a little....commiseration when he acted like he was going to...to *attack* me...which set off Cocoa...which made Tristan go after her. I mean, was I supposed to let that maniac hit my dog with a club?"

"Of course not." Jim dropped a hand to my waist and pulled me close to him. "I'm sorry, Jules. I guess I just feel sorry for the guy. Especially with his disfigurement, I mean, he really can't catch a break."

The sound of Madame C clearing her throat is not unlike the sound of a goose being throttled. A lovely sound and very hard to ignore. Jim immediately moved his hand.

I'm not going to say that the Madame Twins don't like Jim because they do. Or at least they did right up until I stopped seeing Luc and started treating Jim as something more than just a friend.

Madame C barked out a complicated sentence of French at me that she knew I wouldn't be able to follow.

But Jim did.

"What did she say?"

He grinned. "She said you should tell your friend you can't play right now. You have work to do."

"Excuse me, Jim, while I turn and give her one of my most scathing looks."

He laughed. "Nah, never mind. Listen, I saw Theo had a booth serving espressos. How about I go and bring back three cups?"

"Don't bother with *les soeurs*," I said, arching my own eyebrow at Madame C who ignored it. "They wouldn't drink it."

"Because it's from me?"

"Don't take it personally. They're both just being pills."

"How about if I go collect a few samples of the competition?"

"Now you're talking. I'm dying to know if Madame Zabala's éclairs really taste any better."

"Perfect." He gave me a quick kiss on the cheek and headed out into the crowd.

The second he was gone I couldn't help but glance back toward Madame Zabala's booth. When I did I got eye contact with Tristan who was opening up the front shutter on the booth.

Without missing a beat, he made a visually threatening gesture in my direction.

I was astounded. Like it was *my* fault he got arrested for breaking the bakery window!

As Tristan turned away to continue opening up his grandmother's booth, I couldn't help wonder if Chevalier had said something more specific to Tristan to get him so mad but quickly dismissed the idea. Chevalier was an insensitive ass and Tristan hated the world.

That was just a classic bad combination.

7

TOOTH AND NAIL

It took about two seconds for me to tire of standing at the Madame Twins' chocolate éclair booth or thirty minutes in real time. Jim had been gone for ages and I had envious images of him sampling from all the booths and delaying his return. I could hardly blame him.

Both Madame C and Madame B had made it clear that they didn't consider Jim a valid substitute for Luc. While our lack of mutual language comprehension prevented me from explaining to them in detail exactly why I wasn't going to forgive Luc for blocking my escape back to the US last summer, it also prevented *them* from telling me in painstaking detail why they thought I'd made such a colossal mistake with him.

Win-win.

As I leaned against one of the four supporting poles that kept our booth upright I couldn't help notice that the line for éclairs was longest in front of Madame Zabala's booth. I'm sure that seriously annoyed *les soeurs*, especially Madame C who seemed to take particular umbrage at the woman. But hey, you can't argue with people when it comes to pastries. Especially French people.

Madame Zabala had won the contest for best chocolate éclairs for three years running. People wanted the best. Mind you, you'd have to have a pretty refined palate—we're talking Gorden Ramsey on steroids—to be able to tell the difference between one chocolate éclair and another. I mean, unless you'd left the sugar out of one or accidentally substituted cayenne for the vanilla, how could there really be *that* much difference?

Les soeurs were very optimistic about their chances for toppling Madame Zabala from her throne as Queen of the Éclair. Me, I just couldn't imagine there was that much difference between one éclair and another and I was looking forward to Jim's return so I could see for myself.

While I waited—both *les soeurs* were out glad-handing and canvassing as if they were working a political rally, I watched as the Paris judges made their way around the perimeter of the fair tasting various samples of pastries: *palmiers*, croissants, *pain au chocolat*, petit fours, and anything and everything that could be stuffed with cream, custard or chocolate.

Chevalier was in the lead with the other chef, a woman named Enora Roche, I was told, right behind him. Behind both of them hovered the mayor, clearly determined that the two judges would not be upset or insulted in any way.

Ha! Did she know Chevalier at all? He was like a verbal steamroller crushing all good humor in his path. Whatever acerbic, nasty comments he was making as he rounded the pastry contestants' booths were clearly registered on their crestfallen faces as soon as he walked away.

What a jerk. There's no way he can be so good at what he does in Paris to warrant this kind of behavior. What does he even do? Make a really smooth béchamel sauce? Incorporate eggs with one hand tied behind his back? I happen to know—and I don't know much—that all of that sort of donkey work was done by sous chefs and prep cooks.

So where does he get off?

I was startled to see Madame Fournier suddenly in the crowd. She should have had a booth in the festival herself but for whatever reason, she wasn't competing. Her bakery was closed today because—hello!—there were presently more baked goods in this market square than in five bakeries. She probably knew she could count on not even selling a hot dog bun today. Not that she sold hot dog buns. Plus, of course, there was that big ugly board across her broken window from yesterday's debacle.

Just thinking of the broken window reminded me of how the two celebrity chefs had come into the bakery to make a point of humiliating Madame Fournier. I wondered why? Was that just something they typically did? Come into town and head to the nearest bakery to make the proprietor cry?

If the look on Madame Fournier's face was any indication of how she was feeling after that experience, I'd say those chefs had better be mindful of buying any buns from *her* before they left town.

I'm pretty sure the big wad of spittle on top of whatever they bought would be included at no extra charge.

I saw Jim finally heading back to my booth, a cup of coffee in one hand and a white paper bag in the other.

In spite of myself, I felt excitement at the thought of tasting Madame Zabala's famous éclairs. And then immediately afterward guilt like I was betraying *les soeurs*.

"Is that what I think it is?" I said in a loud stage whisper. "Have you tasted one yet?" I asked as I reached for the bag.

Over his shoulder I could see that the two judges were approaching Madame Zabala's booth. I could also see Tristan standing behind the booth with Madame Zabala in front, beaming, ready to greet the two judges.

"I thought we'd do that together," Jim said as I extracted a gooey chocolate éclair from the bag.

Some of the glaze had transferred to the inside of the bag but that wasn't what the judges cared about. Although appearance was important, it all really came down to taste.

Jim set the paper cup of coffee down on the shelf of my booth and stood in front—effectively blocking anyone's view of what we were about to do, although honestly, there was no way they could tell it wasn't one of our own chocolate éclairs.

"There has to be a reason why she wins every year," I said as I held the éclair up and scrutinized it. There was no way this éclair looked any different from the éclairs *les soeurs* and I had been churning out all week long.

"Here goes," I said and bit into it. The custard immediately burst into my mouth and I could tell the chocolate was sharp and rich. Was that the difference? I closed my eyes. The pastry itself was eggy but not overly so.

"Can you taste the difference between hers and the ones the Madame Twins make?" Jim asked.

"It's hard," I said, reluctantly handing the éclair to him. "They're both really good. I'm probably not picking up on the subtle nuances in flavor or whatever."

Jim took two bites before handing it back to me.

"I think I like Madame Zabala's better," he admitted. "But don't tell Madame C. I want to be able to use my kneecaps later in life."

"I might have to agree with you," I said, popping the last bite into my mouth. Was it just because I knew Madame

Zabala had won the contest three years running or was her éclair really better?

"I wonder what her secret ingredient is?" I said, wiping my fingers on a paper napkin.

"Lavender, do you think?"

"I don't know. Probably half the magic would be lost if I knew."

I had to admit it wouldn't be a big surprise if Madame Zabala won again this year. The éclair was that good. Good enough that even I could tell it was better.

Suddenly a scream punched the air behind Jim.

At first, I thought it was part of some kind of street performance. Both chefs were standing in front of Madame Zabala's booth, but Lucien Chevalier was pushing away from the booth and clawing at his throat.

My immediate reaction was that he was just being an ass—attempting to show the world how bad the éclair was he'd just sampled to the point where he wanted to be sick. It was exactly the sort of mean-spirited antic I would expect from him. And that would have fit perfectly except for the fact that Enora Roche was screaming.

And so was the mayor. Either Chevalier was a very good actor and had even fooled his accomplice and the mayor of Chabanel—or he was in trouble.

"Jim, help him!" I shouted as I turned to run out of the back of the booth. By the time I hurried around the side of the booth, Chevalier was on his knees, his eyes bulging, his tongue protruding from his mouth and everyone was standing and staring at him in horror.

Before I could move toward him, Enora Roche let out one long desperate scream.

And Chevalier collapsed at her feet.

8

THE DEVIL'S PLAYGROUND

I have to say I have been personally involved in a few suspicious deaths since I've arrived in Chabanel. After all, I'm a private investigator now. I've even discovered a couple of bodies myself. I've been right next door when the victim was killed. I've even nearly *been* the victim.

But I have never, ever, had someone murdered right before my eyes. Not just *my* eyes—but the whole damn village.

That was a first.

The moment Chevalier fell to the ground, I was beside him. I pulled him onto his back with every intention of giving him mouth to mouth or chest compressions but foam was dribbling out of his mouth and his eyes were glassy and unmoving.

I must have just stared at him because I felt Jim's hand on my arm pulling me away.

"Jules," he said. "He's gone."

Enora Roche was still screaming—although it was much softer now—more like whimpers. But I couldn't take my eyes off Chevalier.

Did he have a bad heart? Or was my initial thought correct?

Had he been murdered in front of all of us?

Let's face it. You meet someone like Lucien Chevalier and then he dies suddenly? The first thing anyone is going to think is that he was murdered. Stands to reason.

"Keep back! Keep back!" Lola Beaufait was saying and I felt Jim tug me more insistently away from the body.

As I got to my feet, I looked at Madame Zabala who was still in her booth, her eyes wide with horror. Beside the booth stood Madame C. There wasn't a single flicker of surprise on her face. But that wasn't unusual. After what she'd endured in her life, she'd probably never be surprised by anything ever again.

"Someone get the police!" Lola said as she moved to Enora and put her arm around the young woman's shoulders. "Immediately! Go!"

As Jim pulled me away, I looked down at the body and saw the chocolate éclair on the ground next to him.

One bite gone.

∽

Luc didn't run. When Monsieur Augustine came to the police station to advise him that there had been an incident at the festival, Luc knew running would only ignite panic.

Matteo and Eloise were both already at the fête. If whatever had happened was so big that *they* couldn't handle it on their own whatever it was must be bad.

The second he approached the square he saw that Matteo had started roping off a large area in front of two food booths. Seeing the body on the ground in front of one of the booths—with no one bothering to give any kind of treatment or medical attention—made him realize he'd been right: a dead body was about as bad as a thing could be.

He pulled the rope up to slip under it and went immediately to the body. Matteo stood nearby with a notebook out, questioning Madame Zabala.

"What happened?" Luc asked.

"It's one of the chef judges down from Paris," Matteo said, glancing at his notes. "Lucien Chevalier. He dropped dead without warning."

Luc noted the éclair on the ground next to the body and glanced at Madame Zabala—her face white, her eyes darting maniacally. Standing next to her were Madame C and Jules. He looked at the other booth within the roped off area and saw Madame B standing behind the counter of that one.

Luc knelt by the body and donned a plastic glove. He touched the man's face. Spittle and foam were clogged around his mouth and his eyes were open. His death had been immediate and violent. He glanced again at the éclair on the ground.

"Who saw this?" he asked.

"Everyone!" Lola Beaufait emerged from the crowd and stepped under the rope. "Everyone saw it. Chef Chevalier was judging Madame Zabala's pastries. He took one bite of the éclair and collapsed!"

Luc glanced at Jules. Had she seen it? In his experience Jules was a remarkably keen observer. If there had been more to see, would she jump in and tell him? He held her eyes for a moment. Behind her, he saw Jim Anderson. The big American stood with his hand on Jules' waist.

"Chief?" Eloise slipped under the rope and stood next to the mayor. "The ME is on his way."

"What are you going to do about this?" Lola said sharply, waving at the crowd, and then at the body.

"Sergeant," Luc said to Eloise. "Get everyone's statements. Matteo, preserve the crime scene. No one comes in. Mayor, I'll ask you to get behind the rope."

"What are you talking about?" Lola gasped as Eloise gently pushed her back toward the rope perimeter. "What do you mean *crime scene*?"

"Everyone!" Luc said, speaking to the gathered crowd as he stood up. "Please line up on the north side of the square to give your statements to my sergeant and then you may leave. The fête is over."

"I'll give my statement right now!" a shrill voice called out.

Luc looked into the crowd to see a young woman, her cheeks streaked with mascara and eyeliner, at the edge of the rope perimeter.

"And you are?" Luc asked, indicating to Eloise that she should interview this witness first.

"I am Enora Roche," the woman said. "Chef Chevalier is my...was my colleague."

"Chef Roche is one of the guest judges invited down from Paris," Lola said stiffly to Luc before going to the woman and putting a comforting arm around her.

"I saw who did this!" Enora Roche said, her eyes overly bright and darting. "I was standing by Lucien when it happened."

"When *what* happened, Madame Roche?" Luc said, narrowing his eyes and trying to determine if this woman was too distraught to be a credible witness.

Enora shot out an arm and pointed at Madame Zabala.

"I was standing next to Lucien when that woman poisoned him!"

9

TESTING THE WATERS

The gasp from the crowd was almost visual the way it built and then crashed like a wave across the square. The terrible words were barely out of Enora Roche's mouth before Matteo—naturally it would be him, the little worm—was clamping hands on poor Madame Zabala and hauling her away.

I could see by Luc's face that he didn't love how things were coming together but I suppose there was an argument to be made that getting Madame Zabala out of the public spotlight was a smart move.

Mayor Beaufait immediately began to attempt to calm Enora who, now that she was witnessing the guilty party being clapped in irons, so to speak, began to pull herself together.

But honestly! Madame Zabala? And the accusation made by a stranger to the village? And not just *any* stranger but one who had been party to some serious ugliness in her brief tenure here?

I was disgusted on top of shocked and was just about to

say so to Jim when I turned to see him looking at me with a decidedly sick expression on his face.

It took me about two seconds to put together the possibly poisoned éclair, the dead chef, and the queasy boyfriend who'd eaten way more of one of Madame Zabala's éclairs than the dead chef had.

I'm quick that way.

"Jim, are you okay?" I said.

His face was white and he'd broken out into a sweat so he'd clearly connected the dots already all by himself.

"I...I'm not sure," he said, looking at the empty pastry bag crumpled up in his hand.

Crap!

I grabbed his arm and was just about to maneuver him to the bench across the square, when Madame Cazaly positioned herself in front of me and pressed a bony but remarkably strong index finger into my shoulder.

"Jules go to police!" she said loudly.

I twisted my shoulder to relieve the uncomfortable poke and attempted to continue walking poor Jim to the bench but Madame C wasn't having it. She slapped my hand away from his shoulder.

"*Now!* Jules go to police *now!*" she said. Madame B was behind her and she was nodding her head.

I rubbed the spot on my shoulder that felt like a power drill bit had gone to work on it.

"What are you talking about?" I said with irritation. "Why would I do that?"

Jim found the bench on his own and his legs collapsed under him. He put his head between his knees. Not a very manly look, I have to say but, I'm sure, completely necessary. I bit my lip as I watched him, my brow wrinkled in concern.

"Madame Zabala needs you! You go now!" Madame C said much louder than anyone needed to be speaking.

"I'm right here, you crazy old bat," I said, fairly sure she couldn't understand my words. "You don't have to shout."

"Jules you go," Madame Becque said, pointing toward the police station.

"Why in the world would I?" I said with exasperation. "You don't even like her. I thought she was your arch enemy."

I watched Jim lift his head. He looked a little better and he gave me a weak thumbs-up sign.

"You must go! You must go!" Madame C shouted, grabbing my arm and pushing me in the direction that both Matteo and Luc had gone with Madame Zabala. A small crowd was listening to every word Madame C was saying.

She spoke a few bits of English but she was saying a whole bunch of French too which I imagine was the same thing only more eloquently.

Bottom line, she wanted me to go to the police station and argue for Madame Zabala's release.

But I still wasn't willing to give up yet. For all I knew Madame Zabala *had* poisoned the chef! After all, the guy had tormented her grandson which ended him up in jail.

"I have an idea," I said brightly. "Why don't we do something totally different for a change and just stay out of it?"

As I watched Jim on the bench it occurred to me that *I'd* had a bite of one of Madame Zabala's éclair too and if the one on the ground that Eloise had stuck in an evidence bag was really the murder weapon, well, it only had a *single* bite taken out of it and that was clearly enough to do the job.

I might as well have saved my breath. Madame C came as close to flipping out as I've ever seen her and I've seen her hold a vintage WWII rifle in her nightgown to a psycho-killer's head so that's saying something.

One thing was sure, I was going to the damn police station, like it or not.

"Fine," I said between gritted teeth. "I'll go. Although why all of a sudden Madame Zabala is your new best friend I have no idea. But I'll go."

I hurried over to where Jim was sitting. His color was a little better and he looked a tad sheepish.

"I'm fine," he said. "It was probably all in my mind. You go on."

"I'll check on you in an hour," I said, putting one hand to his forehead. It was cool and dry.

"Not necessary but yeah, that'd be good."

I gave him a quick kiss and then turned toward the police station.

∽

Tristan watched from the alley as his grandmother was taken away and the police began to rope off her booth.

He couldn't remember a time when he'd felt this happy. Just the sight of her stumbling along trying to keep up with the policeman was a vision he'd call to mind many times in the future when he needed a boost.

He glanced back at the square in time to see someone throwing a sheet over the dead man and again, he felt his affect rise. That bastard dead and the whole village in an uproar made for a pretty perfect day.

As he turned to leave, the money thick and heavy in his pocket, he caught a glimpse of the pretty American girl hurrying away from the square.

In a flash all the pleasure of the day was gone.

This woman, he thought bitterly as he watched her. *This woman* who'd *pitied* him and made him lose his temper! This woman who'd prompted his arrest and humiliation in front of the whole village!

As he watched her go, he knew his time would come to even the score with her.

That was something he knew in his very bones.

10

HARD HEADED

Madame Zabala sat at the small wooden table that Luc's office used as their break table. When not eating pizza or *jambon* sandwiches in this room, they used it as their interview room. Except they rarely had anyone to interview.

After Matteo escorted Madame Zabala to the station, he left to help Eloise finish canvassing and wait for the medical examiner to arrive.

Now that communications, along with transportation, had functionally been thrown back to the eighteen hundreds, it could easily take hours before the doctor arrived. He was coming from Aix and while that was barely five miles away, there was no guarantee he'd have transportation available at a moment's notice.

And until he came the body would have to wait in situ.

Madame Gabin, the police secretary—who had been on an extended vacation for the last few months—came into the interview room with a cup of coffee and set it down in front of Madame Zabala. Madame Gabin had the day off so she could attend the fair but clearly she'd decided things were more interesting at work now.

After she left the room Luc closed the door to the room and sat down across from Madame Zabala.

"I do not even know this chef!" Madame Zabala burst out, her lips trembling.

Luc was fairly sure Madame Zabala had never seen the inside of the *police municipale* in the whole ninety years she'd lived in Chabanel. And now she'd been here twice in one day.

"Was that your éclair on the ground that Monsieur Chevalier had been eating?" Luc asked her as non-threateningly as he could.

"Yes. He sampled it seconds before he…before he…"

"And did he say anything to you *before* sampling the éclair?"

Madame Zabala closed her eyes as if trying to relive the moment when the chef approached her booth. Luc knew Madame Zabala was expected to win the pastry contest as she had the last three years.

If she had a motive to kill the judge, it wasn't at all obvious.

"He…he said my booth smelled like a dead rat," she said, letting out a long breath.

Luc nodded. That was compatible with some of the things he'd heard about Chevalier but it could hardly be considered motive. For one thing, there was not enough time between the man uttering the insult and when Madame Zabala would have needed to "doctor" the pastry to poison him.

This murder had been premeditated.

"Had you spoken to Monsieur Chevalier *before* he approached your booth?"

Madame Zabala's eyes grew wide. "That would be inappropriate!" she said.

She thinks I'm asking her if she tried to influence the judge before he could taste her pastry.

"I meant had you any contact with him at all? At the *boulangerie* yesterday, perhaps?"

"I was not at the *boulangerie* yesterday!"

"Yes, well, any place else? The two judges arrived in Chabanel early yesterday afternoon."

"I never met him before today," she said firmly. "I never spoke to him before today. In fact, I did not speak to him today. I ignored his comment about the smell and when he asked if the éclair was mine, I only nodded."

"And then what happened?"

Madame Zabala threw her hands up in exasperation.

"He made a joke of some kind to the other judge and then she handed him the éclair and he took a small bite."

"Wait. The other judge touched the éclair first?"

"Yes. She was in front of him."

Luc frowned. "Continue, please."

"Then he turned away almost immediately. I remember being surprised because I saw him sample Madame Gravet's beignet and he did not turn away with her beignet in his hand after tasting it. He dropped the beignet back onto the plate in her booth."

"But he didn't do that with your éclair."

"No. He turned away and…well, you know the rest."

"Madame Zabala, did you deliberately poison Lucien Chevalier?"

"What? No! Absolutely not! Never! Not deliberately nor accidentally! My éclairs…everyone in the village has been eating them all morning long!"

Luc watched Madame Zabala's agitation.

Why had Enora Roche accused Madame Zabala? Was it because she was distraught or had she really seen something?

A tap on the door made Luc look up to see Madame Gabin's face in the doorway.

"There is a problem in the waiting room, Chief."

~

I hadn't gotten two steps into the police station when that dildo Adrien Matteo—better known as the French Barney Fife—stopped me.

Where he gets off thinking he can prevent *me*, a Chabanel citizen, from accessing police assistance I do not know but there has literally never been a time when he hasn't given me a hard time for absolutely no reason at all.

Today was no exception.

"You will return to your home," Matteo said, the remnants of his morning's gorge-parade evident down the front of his stained and wrinkled uniform. "We will get a statement from you in due time."

"I'm not here to give a statement," I said.

"Then get out."

"I have every right to be here."

"You have no rights, Madame," he said evenly. "If I ask you to leave a second time, I will lock you up."

"What is your problem, Matteo?"

"Fine. Have it your way."

He grabbed my arm and twisted me around, yanking my other arm behind my back.

I started screaming. Out of the corner of my eye I saw the station secretary jump up and scurry back to wherever I was sure Luc was hiding.

Well, that's not fair. I'm sure he wasn't *hiding* but after being railroaded into this little errand by Madame C, and then bogus-arrested by super-twerp here, I was in no mood to find all the positive attributes of all my ex-friends.

"Be quiet!" Matteo yelled as he handcuffed my wrists.

"Oh, you'd like that, wouldn't you?" I yelled back. "Help! *Au secours! Au secours!*"

"What is going on here?" Luc said as he strode into the waiting room. It occurred to me as he stared at me, my chest heaving with my exertions, my face blotchy from same, that this was the first time we'd seen each other in five weeks.

I was not looking my best.

"Matteo, uncuff her," Luc growled. "Do we not have enough to do today?"

"But Chief..."

Matteo clearly wasn't going to give up that easy but he did twist me around so he could at least pretend to be unlocking the handcuffs.

"What are you doing here?" Luc said to me, his blue eyes glittering but otherwise showing no sign of what he was feeling.

"I am here to represent Madame Zabala," I said, breathlessly.

"You are not a lawyer."

"I'm here to represent her nonetheless," I said as I felt the cuffs finally release. I shot Matteo a sullen look and then rubbed my wrists as if I'd been hung up by them for hours. I've learned it never hurts for people to think you're hurt worse than you are especially if you're even mildly in the wrong.

Before Luc had a chance to react to my comment Lola Beaufait rushed into the station and, ignoring all of us, went straight to Luc.

"Where is the suspect?" she said. "It is my responsibility

to ensure that our guest is safe from any further attacks. Is Madame Zabala behind bars?"

"Madame Zabala didn't kill anyone," I said hotly although as soon as the words were out of my mouth I knew that I really had no idea if she had or hadn't.

"Instead of wasting everyone's time with some little old lady," I said, "why don't you focus on finding the real killer?"

Honestly I'm not sure who I was speaking to at this point. Ostensibly I was replying to Lola but since she wasn't the one tasked with finding Chevalier's killer, I guess I was talking to Luc. Only it had been so long, and my emotions were still so jumbled about him, that I really was talking more to the room than specifically to him.

In any case, Luc ignored me. He turned to Matteo, his eyes hooded and his face unreadable. "Finish canvassing the witnesses," he said.

"Why bother with that?" Lola said in frustration. "A witness has given you the identity of the culprit. Served up on a silver plate with a doily!"

"And Matteo?" Luc said, ignoring the mayor.

Matteo stopped half way out the door. "Yes?" he said tightly.

I could tell he was pissed at having to let me go. But it was more than that. I'm not sure why I never saw it before but in that split second I saw clearly something that was as true as the sky being blue and sunflowers yellow and that was that Matteo didn't like Luc.

Not one bit.

And I'd never noticed it before. I'd spent some time wondering why Luc kept Matteo on although I knew it was because Luc was short-handed. It never occurred to me that Matteo wasn't thrilled with the arrangement either.

"Once the ME is onsite," Luc said to Matteo, "have Eloise bring Enora Roche to the station for questioning."

Matteo glanced at Lola, as well he might. She literally ignited at Luc's words.

"What are you talking about? You've already heard what she had to say! Are you mad? Are you trying to ensure that Chabanel is cooking its food over a campfire for the next ten years? No! I forbid it!"

But Matteo had already left.

"I don't know what you think you're doing," Lola said, getting as close to Luc's face as I'd ever seen anybody do who wasn't about to plant a big juicy one on them. "But I will not allow you to jeopardize the relationship that I have worked so hard to—"

"Lola, sit down," Luc said tiredly, indicating the waiting room. "I'll be happy to talk with you in a moment. Madame Gabin!"

The station secretary stood up from her desk in the receptionist alcove and watched the mayor sputtering and pacing in the waiting room.

"Yes, Chief?" Madame Gabin said, pursing her lips in distaste.

"Get the mayor a coffee, please." He looked over at me. "You come with me."

I'll always wonder what he had in mind for me and I've given it some thought since then but I was not to know—not then at least—because right then whatever Luc had in mind for me was completely thwarted by the opening of the front door.

Sergeant Eloise Basille entered leading yet another poor little old lady in hand cuffs.

This time it was none other than Madame Léa Cazaly.

11

THE LESS YOU KNOW

Marie Fournier stood at her sink in her flat above the *boulangerie* and washed her hands. Initially she had decided to wash them because they were shaking so badly she didn't know what else to do with them.

An image of Lady Macbeth came to mind as she fought down a nervous giggle.

A very big part of her still couldn't believe what she'd done. Still couldn't believe her incredible bravery. And her reward had been instantaneous.

She'd never felt more alive!

And wasn't that ironic? With Lucien Chevalier now dead?

A rush of delight trembled through her, spoiled only by the fleeting memory of poor old Madame Zabala being hauled away for the crime.

And then even that image prompted a chortle—unladylike though it was—that she literally could not hold back.

Oh, what a day. What a wonderful, exceptional day.

Her eye fell on the small packet of rat poison on her

shelf and the glee drained from her as the practical side of her took over. She'd bought the poison for the mice she'd found in the supply room but now she snatched the packet up and emptied its contents down the drain, pouring a cup of water after to hurry it on its way to the sewers.

No sense in tempting fate.

Or making the gendarmes' job easier for them.

∽

I'm trying to think if I've ever seen Luc so frustrated. As a matter of fact I have but it was hard to tell since I was pretty frustrated myself.

"What the hell is going on?" I said to Eloise. "Why is Madame Cazaly in handcuffs?"

To her credit Eloise looked ashamed of herself but she didn't answer me. She looked at her boss, and swallowed hard.

"She insisted I bring her in," she said.

"In handcuffs?" I said loudly, slapping my hand against my slacks in frustration. I felt Luc's hand on my arm as he pulled me away from Eloise and Madame C and gave me a none too gentle push in the direction of the waiting room where I had to quickly sidestep to avoid colliding with the mayor who had jumped to her feet.

"She insisted I cuff her," Eloise said to Luc. "It was easier to do it than convince her otherwise."

Ha. Welcome to my world, I thought.

"Are there any *other* little old ladies you need to arrest today?" I said to Luc. "I hear the old folks home is just a few streets over. I'm sure there are a few potential felons there you could slap in irons."

"Be quiet," Luc growled at me. "You're making it worse."

"I'm not sure that's possible," I said. But when Luc turned and gave me a steely look, I decided to put a lid on the quips at least until I found out what was going on. That was my plan, anyway, but as soon as I saw the smug look on Madame C's face, I couldn't follow through.

"You couldn't give me fifteen minutes to try to spring Madame Zabala?" I said to her. "Why did you send me here in the first place if you intended to pull this stunt?"

Madame C shrugged, obviously determined only to give name, rank and serial number. *If this was the game she wanted to play I had a half a mind to let them have her.*

"Did you arrest her?" Luc asked Eloise.

"No, Chief. I just asked her to come for questioning because..."

To Eloise's credit, she looked around the room as if concerned about whether or not she should be blabbing case details to a public waiting room.

"Because someone reported seeing me tamper with Madame Zabala's éclairs," Madame Cazaly said to Luc. "It was during the time when Madame Zabala was at the police station obtaining her grandson's release."

I turned to Eloise. "Who said they saw her? Madame C has the right to face her accuser."

"Jules, I will personally escort you out of this office if you don't be quiet," Luc said, his even temper clearly threatening to give way any moment.

"Madame Cazaly couldn't have tampered with anything at Madame Zabala's booth," I said hotly, ignoring his warning. "She was with me the whole time!"

"*Non*, Jules, you were busy walking around the fair with the unemployed American," Madame C said.

Really? Even in the middle of a murder investigation you can't give Jim a break?

"Besides, my sister will confirm that I was in fact at Madame Zabala's booth," Madame C said. "I am afraid I could not bear the thought that she would win four years in a row."

"You are confessing?" Luc and I asked together in astonishment.

"*Exactement.*"

12

A NECESSARY EVIL

To say my mouth fell open when Madame C made her big confession would not be hyperbole. In fact, I was so stunned—and really, I've known her long enough that I shouldn't have been—that Luc found it very easy to take me by the arm, lead me out the front door and give me a little push that put me—still open-mouthed with shock—onto the street in front of the police station.

Unbelievable!

Just before Luc tossed me out Madame C gave me a look that conveyed her meaning more clearly than her broken English ever could. And then she spoke, her voice raspy with emotion: "Don't forget to feed the goats tonight!"

So yeah, I will cherish that memory always.

I stood outside the station and totted up what I knew about what had just happened.

One of the Paris judges had dropped dead after tasting Madame Zabala's éclair. The other judge had accused Madame Zabala of poisoning the man. Someone *else* had accused Madame C of doing it. Both old ladies were in custody. And one—the crazier one—had confessed to killing him.

I straightened my tunic. Yep, that about covered it.

Since Madame B was marginally the less crazy of the two sisters, and since Madame C seemed to think her sister would support her claim, I figured I needed to head back to the fair to see if I could get some semblance of the truth out of Madame B.

One thing was sure. Between Madame Zabala and Madame Cazaly, Luc was going to get precisely nada for all his interrogation techniques.

That much I knew was true.

I hurried across the square *de la maire* and turned down one of the side alleys that ran parallel to the fair. It wasn't the most direct route back but weirdly like most village layouts in France it still qualified as a short cut. As I came out the end of the nearest alley, I could see across the street at Café Sucre. I knew that even now most people were at the fair. Even the owner of the Café Sucre, Theo Bardot, was at the fair.

Which is why it was so easy to spot Tristan in the outdoor café eating a meal. I was so surprised to see him that I literally stopped in my tracks.

He sat in the middle of the café surrounded by assorted dishes and beer bottles. He was the only customer in the place and was happily chowing down with a single-minded focus that I must say is singular to the French when it comes to food.

But one would have thought perhaps his behavior inappropriate on the day his only living relative was hauled off to jail on suspicion of murder.

Was this weird? I wondered as I walked past the café toward where the fair was—another two blocks away. Was it weird that Tristan would be having an elaborate meal at a café *now* of all times? Where did he get the money? And where was *he* doing the critical time period?

But most of all I wondered, *how can he just sit there stuffing his face when his grandmother has been arrested?*

I had very little time to obsess about Tristan's attributes as a grandson because as I came to where the fête was I saw that the police had pushed everyone further away from the body and the crime scene so that the closest I could get was the far perimeter of the fair.

I saw the ambulance immediately because it was such an oddity to see a working vehicle these days. And also because it was large and ancient. Several other uniformed police and medical personnel had joined Matteo and Romeo—the retired detective who worked part-time at the station—who were combing through both Madame Zabala's booth and our own. What they were doing looked more like contaminating the crime scene than processing it but I suppose that's small town forensic science in post-EMP France.

I spotted Madame B standing nearby. I immediately went to her and put my arm around her.

"Oh, Jules, tout va bien avec Léa?"

"Oh sure, Justine," I said, patting her shoulder. "Léa is just peachy. You did know she confessed to killing a man, right?"

Madame B shook her head—not in denial—but as if she couldn't quite understand me.

And *that* I know was not true at all.

"Tell me what's going on," I said firmly. "Why did Léa say she poisoned the chef?"

"Because she did?" Madame B said meekly.

I snorted. "Why would she want to kill him? She didn't even know him!"

"I don't pretend to know all my sister's secrets."

"Quit being so cryptic!" I literally felt my muscles quiver in agitation. "Léa didn't kill Chevalier and you know it so why are you okay with her confessing to it? Who are you two protecting?"

Madame B shrugged and looked back as the ambulance, now carrying the body, revved its engine and slowly made its way through the crowd of pedestrians.

"My English is not being so good," she murmured as she watched the ambulance leave.

I crossed my arms in front of my chest and swore I could feel my blood pressure inching upward. Finally I turned and left her there—to gossip and pretend to be shocked with her neighbors—to go check on Jim.

~

Luc stood in the hall of the police station after ushering Madame Cazaly into his office and leaving her there. They had no holding facility fit for someone of her age. Luc had no doubt she'd want something a little more jail-like for whatever point it was she was trying to make.

He reflected on how he felt seeing Jules again after so many weeks of only seeing her from a distance. He couldn't help notice how passionate she looked when she was angry.

And how beautiful.

"So Madame Cazaly really confessed?" Matteo said leaving the front desk alcove where he'd clearly gotten this info from Madame Gabin. "What is she? A hundred years old?"

"Ninety-three," Luc said. "I'm not sure what it was. It

wasn't recorded. When I asked her what poison she used, she said arsenic."

"But Chevalier wasn't poisoned with arsenic," Matteo said.

While it would be weeks before they knew exactly what poison had been used, one thing they were able to determine was that *whatever* had been inserted into the lethal chocolate éclair had a distinct smell to it. Arsenic was odorless and didn't kill instantaneously in small doses.

"I'm pretty sure she has no idea what she is saying," Luc said.

"But you still intend to question her," Matteo said. It wasn't a question.

"I intend for us to find the person responsible for this murder," Luc said tersely. "If you think becoming distracted by an old woman's silliness is the best way to do that..."

"Why are we indulging her then?" Matteo said, frowning in the direction of Luc's office.

"Because it costs us nothing to do so. Where is Madame Roche?"

Matteo shrugged. "Mayor Beaufait said the woman will give a statement from her hotel room."

"Oh, she said that?"

It was interesting to note that of all the people that Matteo took absolutely no guff from—and the list was long—Lola Beaufait, the very picture of bureaucracy, could get him to do back flips.

Lola was in her fifties perhaps even older. But she was still beautiful.

Even so, Matteo's response irritated Luc.

Does Lola truly think she can salvage this disaster? Does she think for one moment that kid-gloving the surviving chef will make any difference at all?

"Where are the rest of the éclairs now?" Luc asked.

"They've been sent to the lab."

"All of them?"

"Yes, of course."

Luc knew Matteo didn't like him any more than Luc liked him. It made every interaction between them twice as hard as it needed to be.

"What will you do with Madame Zabala now that you have a confession?" Matteo asked.

"I've already released her. If we need her, we know where to find her."

Luc knew Matteo wanted to argue with that. Wisely, for a change, he didn't.

Matteo turned away just as Romeo and Eloise burst into the station. Luc wondered with annoyance who was minding the crime scene.

"We found the poison," Romeo said, nodding at Eloise who held a large cardboard box.

Matteo and Luc joined them. Inside the box was a paper bag filled to the brim with dozens of plants.

Luc recognized it immediately. Foxglove. A deadly poison, its fragrance was pungent and bitter.

Ingesting enough of it could cause instant death.

"Where did you find it?"

"The sack was left in the open where anyone could see," Eloise said breathlessly, clearly excited at her discovery.

"Yes," Luc said patiently. "And where was that?"

Eloise hesitated and then glanced down the hall toward the room where they were holding Madame Cazaly.

Surely, not, Luc thought, his heart sinking.

"We found it inside *les soeurs*' pastry booth," Romeo said.

13

THE BEST LAID PLANS

I have to say that Jim lives in one of the coolest places in Chabanel.

First his building is situated on a narrow dark street near the edge of town. I always assumed the villagers built this part last because wouldn't you start in the middle of your town and build outward? So it makes sense that this street and the buildings on it would be more recent than the rest of Chabanel.

Mind you, it's still medieval. Big time. If you've ever been to France you know what I'm talking about. The fact that nobody's bulldozed this street and thrown up prefabs or doublewides or even a line of tiny houses is seriously a mystery. I'm not saying the French are lazy or anything. Let's just say they like their history and leave it at that.

Anyway, you walk down this cramped little street until you come to a massive mahogany door—one of those doors that looks like it belongs on a castle. Behind the door is a good size courtyard. It's totally pavered with a nonworking three-tiered stone fountain with a cherub statue in the middle of the top tier peeing into the water. Very classy.

All around the courtyard are shuttered windows with flower boxes and climbing vines.

Across the courtyard there was a stone archway—again hinting at the semblance of a castle—that you go through and a little alcove with one door painted high gloss blue.

I knocked on the door and wondered how long before Jim got around to offering me a key. We haven't actually done anything, if you know what I mean, but I do think it would be a nice gesture.

He answered the door like he'd been waiting for me. Dear Jim. He probably had.

"Hey, you're looking better," I said, stepping into his apartment. He'd changed clothes so I worried that might have been because he'd thrown up on himself. "How do you feel?"

He grinned in embarrassment. "Like an idiot. I can't believe I thought I'd been poisoned too. What a moron."

"Jim, no, not at all," I said as I gave him a hug. "A guy drops dead eating an éclair from the same tray you'd just eaten from? It was perfectly reasonable."

"Well, *you* didn't freak out."

"I didn't because I didn't eat as much as you and also because I had my hands full dealing with the crazy twins."

"Yeah, what's happening?"

We moved into his living room and he went to get a pitcher of lemonade. He's such a perfect host. I wish the Madame Twins could see him on his own turf. They'd be so impressed. I always forget to offer people a drink when they come to *La Fleurette*.

"Well, you saw they took Madame Zabala in for questioning." I said.

"That's just idiotic. I hope they've released her by now."

"I don't know but probably soon since Madame C stepped forward to confess to killing the guy."

Jim stopped, with one hand holding my glass of lemonade, his mouth open in shock.

"You have got to be kidding me. Why would she do that?"

"That is the question I ask every single day in relation to Madame C." I took the lemonade and set it down on the coffee table while Jim pulled out a stack of coasters. "I tried asking Madame B but she's no help."

"Do you think Madame Zabala might know?" Jim sat down on the couch.

"Maybe. Surely she saw *something* before all this happened."

"Where was her grandson?"

"Good question. I don't know. But I know where he was moments after his grandmother was arrested." I quickly filled Jim in on seeing Tristan at Café Sucre.

Jim shook his head in disgust. "What is his problem?"

"Madame B says he hates the world. But she says he has good reason too."

"The hair lip?"

"Presumably. But with Madame B, it's not always obvious. She may know something of his history."

"You mean him being the illegitimate son of a gypsy?"

"You have gossip about Tristan?" Jim's French was fluent so it stood to reason he'd pick up stuff around town that would fly over my head.

"I hate to gossip," Jim said with a frown.

And I hate the fact that I used the word *gossip* just as he was about to spill his guts to me.

"Come on, Jim. Poor old Madame C is sitting in a jail cell right this minute and you and I both know Tristan is a better fit as the killer. I mean he had a violent altercation with the dead man just the night before. And he was there at the scene of the crime. He could easily have doctored the éclair. So what do you know about him?"

Jim shifted uncomfortably. I could tell he didn't like telling stories out of school but honestly I always thought men were worse than women when it came to spreading gossip. I can tell he wants to tell me what he knows.

"Okay, but this is just rumor," he said.

"Spill it."

"I heard that Tristan is the only child of Madame Zabala's only daughter—a wild girl who ran off with a gypsy forty years ago and got pregnant."

"But Tristan is too young to be that baby."

"Exactly. The gossip I heard was *that* baby was a girl. And *she* went the way of her mother and her grandmother and got pregnant in her twenties."

"So Tristan is Madame Zabala's great-grandson?"

"I guess."

"Okay, well, why does he act like he hates her?"

"I don't know. It's a pretty tough hand he's been dealt. You couldn't blame him for being bitter."

"And murderous?"

"He does seem to lack control. But wouldn't you say this murder was all about control? And planning? Tristan strikes me as a blunt force trauma kind of guy."

"I think you're right," I said with a sigh. "It's too finessed for him. But still. All the other pieces fit."

"What are you going to do?"

I picked up my lemonade. It was chilly outside and I'd have preferred something hot but the only thing harder than being a good host was being a good guest.

"Well, I know from past experience it's a waste of time

trying to talk Madame C out of whatever she's set her mind on doing. And besides, I don't know if I mentioned it but someone in the village claimed they saw her messing around in Madame Zabala's booth when it was vacant."

"Seriously?"

"Well, I didn't see it, but somebody claimed they did."

Jim grinned. "And I know from past experience that you've already got a plan for how to derail Madame C's best laid intentions."

I couldn't help but laugh even though I felt more fretful than jolly. I don't know why the Madame Twins always have to make everything so hard. It seems like everything I do to take care of them involves going through major roadblocks that *they* have set up. Is that a French thing, I wonder? Or just a Léa and Justine thing?

"I think I'm going to talk to everyone at the fair," I said as the thought came to me. "The other booth operators, the other chef judge—"

"And Luc?"

Jim said it casually but I know the subject of Luc was anything but casual with him. I chose my words carefully.

"I don't know how helpful Luc will be at this point," I said. "I'm sure he knows that Madame C didn't kill anyone but he's not going to upset her further by not taking her seriously. It's all a kind of game. And frankly I feel sorry for him because he has to go through the motions of treating it as real."

"Are you sure he doesn't believe her confession? That would make his job a whole lot easier."

"Luc knows Madame C," I said, fighting back annoyance. Why was Jim making me defend Luc? I don't want to think of Luc's positive traits at the moment. "Luc was a regular visitor to *La Fleurette* until...recently," I said.

"I remember," Jim said dryly.

See, this is exactly what I *didn't* want to happen. I haven't said two sentences to Luc in five weeks and here he is wedging himself between me and Jim without even trying.

"What about Tristan?" Jim asked. "Do you really need to talk to him? He sounds dangerous."

What is it with the guys I date? They're all so paternalistic and protective. Very sweet until you actually have to spend the extra time and energy to work around it.

"Jim, I have to talk to Tristan too."

"He'll just lie if he doesn't out and out assault you."

"I can take care of myself."

"Forgive me if those sound like famous last words. How about if I come with you?"

"Thank you, but no. You're too tall. You'll intimidate people."

"On the plus side, I speak the language."

"Hey, I'm getting better!" I said, scooting over to him on the couch. "Nowadays I only sound like a slow-witted toddler."

He laughed and kissed me.

"At least you're under no illusions about your skill level," he said with a grin.

~

Tristan felt the sweat bead up on his brow and then slowly drip down his face onto his shirt. He'd followed the American down this street and was able to spot her until she slipped behind the large wooden door in the middle of the street. Naturally he didn't dare follow her any further but watching and waiting for her in the alley was nearly as dangerous.

There was nothing to hide behind. Not even a rain barrel.

He hurried to the end of the alley and was gratified to see that it emptied out into a vacant crossroads—a line of uninhabited houses on the one side faced a line of abandoned shops on the other.

Knowing that the American would have to either come this way or the way she'd come—and either way he'd see her—Tristan slipped into the stone alcove of a boarded up entranceway. Someone had gotten sick on the threshold, but not recently, and garbage had piled up in the inner recesses. But whatever had been organic had long since lost its foul smell.

Not that bad smells bothered Tristan. Not a bit.

Nor did standing and waiting. He'd spent half his childhood doing exactly that.

When it came to exacting vengeance on those who'd harmed him...

...he could wait forever.

14

WINGING IT

You're going to think I'm paranoid but when I left Jim's place I could not shake the feeling that I was being followed. I did look behind me a few times and not surprisingly saw nothing. Mind you, if someone really was following me, unless they were total hopeless, they'd probably do everything to ensure I didn't notice them.

It helped talking everything over with Jim. I've found in the past few months when I've been involved in these sorts of cases that I need someone to bounce ideas off. Amazingly, things you know in your head sometimes take on a whole different meaning when you speak them out loud.

In any case, I walked back to the fair to see that only the police were left wandering around the square now. The yellow tape that encompassed both Madame Zabala and Madame C's booths fluttered in the chill breeze.

Madame Becque had obviously gone home. Or possibly not. It was just as likely she'd ridden her bike to Aix to confess to some crime happening over there. I wouldn't put it past her.

I saw Matteo and Luc standing by the booths talking and while it made me think that now might be a good time to have another conversation with Madame C while the cats were away, I was surprised to realize I didn't have the energy for it.

It was just as well. I was sure I wouldn't find out anything Madame C didn't want me to and I'd been down enough dead ends for one day.

My conversation with Jim did make me want to track down Tristan Zabala sooner rather than later though. And talking with him in a public place—like say a café—would be a wise plan.

Happy with this thought, I hurried back to Café Sucre, passing Madame Fournier's *boulangerie* en route. The front window was still boarded up but I caught a glimmer of light coming from inside. I figured Madame Fournier must be in there pounding dough or growing yeast or something.

One thing was for sure: with the sudden closing of the pastry festival, her croissants and beignets would be in high demand tomorrow. I imagine she'd want to skip the chocolate éclairs, though. At least for a few days.

As soon as I reached the café, I scanned the outdoor area and saw what I should have known: Tristan was no longer there. It had been a long shot anyway. Not too disappointed, since honestly, how could anyone look forward to a confrontation with Tristan? I decided to take a seat and treat myself to a late afternoon *espresso*. Something warm to counter the effects of the iced drink Jim had given me.

Theo Bardot, the owner of Café Sucre, brought me an espresso without my having to ask which either meant he was getting to know me and my preferences or that was all he had in the way of beverages today. Life after the EMP had taken many different forms here in the south of France, and the confidence that we would get what we ordered at any café or restaurant since the disaster was one of them.

"*Merci*, Theo," I said as he set down my tiny demitasse cup. "Quite the excitement today."

Theo was one of the few villagers who spoke decent English and I tended to seek him out as a result. He'd done a year in a student exchange program in California a few decades ago and was rightfully proud of the language skills he'd hung onto.

"It is a terrible thing," Theo said, shaking his head. I always thought he looked like the archetypical French waiter. He was tall, with a mustache and wore suit slacks and a white shirt and tie with a long white apron. Thanks to the Madame Twins I knew only too well how difficult it was to press linens these days so I had to admire the effort Theo went to for his appearance.

"Has Madame Zabala been released yet, do you know?" I asked.

Theo was second only to the barkeep for knowing the most recent news in the village. And since the barkeep was presently in jail for attempting to murder a police officer last month and his bar closed for business, Theo was our CNN and *Le Monde* all rolled into one.

"*Non*, but soon, I understand, now that Madame Cazaly has taken her place."

Theo didn't say that at all ironically. After all these years he must be beyond the point where the twins could surprise him.

"I noticed Madame Zabala's great-grandson was in your café right after it all happened," I said.

He nodded. I shouldn't have been surprised that he knew. I think his nephew or stepson waited tables when Theo wasn't around.

"It is true," he said with disgust. "And where did the *cochon* get the money? I will tell you where. He stole it from his grandmother. *Connard!*"

"Yeah, he definitely strikes me as an opportunist," I said, wondering if Theo knew the gossip about Tristan. "Does he live with Madame Zabala?"

Theo frowned at that and glanced away. "I do not think so," he said. "He is rarely in the village, preferring to stay in *Mégisseries* with the rest of the rats."

I knew *Mégisseries*. I'd actually had cause to visit there when I first moved to Chabanel and it was not one of the highlights of my month.

"The main black market for Chabanel is set up there now," Theo continued. "I go when I must."

He meant when he runs out of sugar or chocolate. Unlike some of the more notorious black markets in Provence, *Mégisseries* was largely for hard-to-find food items.

At least that's what I've been told.

I finished my coffee and thanked Theo for the conversation. The afternoon air had gotten mean and I was sorry I'd left my heavier jacket at home. I flipped up the collar on my denim jacket and headed back to *La Fleurette*.

It was too late to visit *Mégisseries* today—I wouldn't risk getting caught there after dark—and besides, there were the damn goats to feed.

∽

Adele Zabala unlocked her front door and hesitated. Would he be here? She heard nothing inside and when she entered she saw no evidence that her great grandson had been here. She relaxed and walked to her kitchen.

Without taking her jacket off she went to her antique

porcelain jar and pried the lid off. Looking around as if the walls might see, she slipped her hand in the jar and touched the coins inside.

She felt a shimmer of relief. He hadn't found her pin money.

Satisfied, she took her coat off and hung it on the peg by the kitchen door that led to the garden and then went to the stove. It had been placed next to her electric cooker. Keeping the now useless stove made her kitchen much smaller but she didn't have the heart to remove it and besides, if she did, she would be giving in and accepting that this was the way she must live now.

And she would never give in. Never.

She lit the tinder and set the tea kettle on top of the woodstove. It would be easily a quarter of an hour before the water was hot enough for tea.

But Agathe was used to waiting to get what she wanted.

While she waited, she straightened up her already tidy kitchen and wondered if the chef hadn't died if she would have won the contest again this year.

She set out a heavy crock mug and pulled out the tin of tea leaves. As she scooped the leaves into the mug she wondered why Léa Cazaly would confess to a crime that any fool could see she didn't commit?

She shook her head and glanced out the back kitchen window to the garden and wondered where that useless mongrel Tristan was.

If she had any luck at all perhaps he might finally be gone for good.

15

DETAILS, DETAILS

The next morning, I woke up at dawn's early crack and still I didn't beat Madame B downstairs. Before I could throw back the duvet on my bed, I heard her downstairs rattling the pots and pans. The delightful smell of coffee drifted up to me. Cocoa lifted her head from where she slept at the foot of my bed as if smelling coffee was her cue to desert me.

Well, she *is* a French dog but I'm pretty sure it has more to do with the fact that she knew there would be éclairs to go *with* the coffee.

"Yes, go on," I said and she shot off the bed, her nails making clicking sounds on the centuries-old tiles in the hall and stairs. Once she was gone I could see that one of the cats—the black one named Neige—was curled up on a chair in my bedroom.

No amount of coaxing or éclairs would get *her* downstairs unless she had a mind to go. I knew she'd been out hunting vols and mice all night and wouldn't deign to descend to walk amongst us mere mortals until nearer to *apéro* time.

I showered and dressed for my visit to *Mégisseries*. On the one hand I was hoping to find Tristan and question him in his natural environment. Failing that, I would settle for talking to anyone who knew him.

It wasn't much but it was either that or try again to get the truth out of one of the Madame Twins.

I hurried downstairs to see Madame Becque on her hands and knees polishing the kitchen floor. This was very strange behavior even for her.

"I'm going into town," I said as I picked up a stale croissant and poured a cup of coffee for myself.

Madame B looked up. "Will you visit Léa?"

"Why? Think she'll tell me why she's doing this if I do?"

Something passed across Madame B's face when I said that and I think it was the first sign of impatience with me. That's saying something for Justine Becque.

Mother Theresa would lose her cool before Madame B did.

I decided not to push it. The two sisters had their reasons. Fine. It was only a murder confession.

Probably won't even get life if you're in your nineties.

"I'll be back around lunchtime," I said.

She nodded and turned back to her work.

The black market was situated at the far end of the rue de Carmes in *Mégisseries*. The last time I'd been here was five months ago—right after the EMP happened. I had every reason to believe that the place had solidified since then. What had before been a decaying collection of seedy, abandoned store fronts and a few inebriated people staggering around could very well be a wild west town of prospering ignominy and greed by now.

I had no idea what to expect.

I took my bike since it was at least two miles on the other side of Chabanel and *La Fleurette* was already three miles outside of town. I know that doesn't seem like a lot but it's right at my limit. I was wearing eggplant colored driving mocs, skinny jeans under a flouncy print skirt, a thermal turtleneck and a cashmere cardigan. In case I went missing I definitely wanted people to remember they saw me.

The village of Chabanel rises early and even though it wasn't yet eight in the morning, the streets were already busy with shoppers and kids making their way to school. I drove my bike slowly, passing the square the fête had been on and saw that the only thing left now was the yellow police tape. The police had gone.

It didn't take long to break free of the neighborhoods and streets of the center of the village.

When I first came to Chabanel someone told me *Mégisseries* meant tanneries—basically meaning that even back in the Middle Ages *Mégisseries* had been the bad side of town.

As I drew closer to where I thought the black market was set up, a part of me—a very big part of me—began to feel sorry that I didn't take Jim up on his offer to come with me.

~

As Luc walked to the Chabanel hotel, the thought came to him that few things could make a man feel more like a lap dog than doing the bidding of a delusional woman with no interest in preserving justice or following due process.

So why was he paying attention to Lola Beaufait's wants and desires? She was so wrapped up with her belief that this remaining judge might provide good public relations for

Chabanel that she'd completely skipped over the fact that the other judge had been murdered in Chabanel.

Did I mention delusional?

And yet keeping peace in Chabanel often started with keeping peace with the mayor. It was a hard lesson to learn and Luc was still struggling to learn it.

On the other hand, especially in the grand scheme of things, it didn't cost him much to take Enora Roche's statement in her hotel instead of at the station.

Until any sort of facts came back from the lab that they could actually use, Luc had to admit he was stalled on the murder investigation. It was mildly problematic that the person confessing to the crime had means and opportunity—and the murder weapon had been found in her booth.

Luc's job now was not just to find the killer but to prove the innocence of someone who did not want to be proven innocent.

Is this really the job I signed on for? Working twelve hour days, seven day weeks, no sleep, no real financial incentive, fighting the mayor every step of the way—for what?

Luc struggled to shake off his discouragement.

Seeing Jules with Anderson yesterday didn't help.

He marched up the steps of the hotel, not bothering to acknowledge Bonnet on the front desk.

Finding the Foxglove in Madame C's booth was problematic on many different levels. But if you believed her innocence, as Luc did, then you were left with the fact that someone had put it there. And who besides the real killer would have done that?

When he'd asked her how the Foxglove came to be in her booth she tried to make up a reason but the day before she hadn't even known the real poison—*arsenic indeed*—so he hadn't expected to get anything useful from the conversation.

And he hadn't.

Luc bounded up the stairs to the second floor and forced himself to focus on the task at hand. He went to room twenty-two and knocked firmly. Lola Beaufait answered the door.

Why am I surprised?

"I am here to take Madame Roche's statement," Luc said.

"Madame Roche is very upset at the moment," Lola said. Behind her Luc could see Enora Roche sitting at a dressing table watching them.

"So you're saying this is not a good time?" Luc said, barely keeping his tone civil.

Lola turned to look at Enora and then back at Luc.

"I think in the morning might be better. Besides, don't you already have a suspect in custody?"

Luc gently pushed past Lola to stand in front of Enora. "Madame Roche? Do you need medical assistance?"

"She's not *sick*, Luc!" Lola said with annoyance. "She's *upset* by what happened. Surely you can understand that."

"Is that true, Madame?" Luc said. "You are emotionally upset?"

Enora Roche looked at Luc with terrified eyes and nodded mutely. It was the strangest reaction to a perfectly innocent question Luc had ever seen.

Especially from someone with nothing to hide.

He glanced around the room and then nodded curtly. "Tomorrow, then," he said and let himself out.

As he walked out into the crisp autumn air he didn't know much but he knew one thing.

Enora Roche looked as guilty as he had ever seen a person look.

The big scary black market looked like a big non-scary flea market.

Not even that big.

As I stood next to my bike, I tried to see how it was that different from the daily markets in Aix or even Chabanel.

True, the Chabanel market didn't have truffles or *foie gras*. Or absinthe. Or real silk negligees. Or Veuve Cliquot. And at the prices that *Mégisseries* sellers were asking for most of these items, there was a good reason why not.

Normal people couldn't afford six hundred euros for a bottle of champagne that just six months ago only cost fifty. Or a hundred euros for a starter dish that every café and brasserie in the country offered for five euros back in the spring.

Months ago Katrine had told me that this market didn't use strictly cash and while she'd hinted that prostitution was a going concern here, what she *hadn't* mentioned—and which was plain to see by all the small curtained kiosks—was that it was also an acceptable method of payment for goods.

The first time I saw a woman emerge from one of the curtained booths, buttoning her trousers and reaching for the small bag of truffles she'd just "purchased," I wanted to gasp like Hester Prynne.

There were at least a hundred people milling about and shopping. Most of them had wicker or plastic carry-alls. The people in the booths didn't look all that scary; just maybe a little rough around the edges. They'd been poor before the EMP. They were a lot less poor now because of the market. I'm sure they still weren't welcome to move into Chabanel.

I walked my bike the length of the market and then

A Bad Éclair Day

stopped in front of one of the little curtained changing rooms—for lack of an immediately cruder word for them—but saw no trace of Tristan. What I did see was a lot of eyes on me.

Unfriendly eyes. Men's eyes.

All of a sudden I wished I hadn't worn the skirt over the jeans. And purple loafers? Am I just starved for attention?

I kicked a little dirt on my shoes to make them a little less...purple.

"You are new here?"

I turned to see a young woman with pockmarked skin. She was clearly bra-less and slightly overweight. But she was smiling. And she spoke English.

"How did you know I was American?" I asked, grateful to have someone to talk to. As soon as I engaged her, I felt the men's eyes turn away from me.

"Oh, I didn't. I can't tell English from American. So you are American?"

I nodded and glanced at the curtained cubicle behind her. There didn't seem to be anybody in it. She turned and gave a dazzling smile to a man who walked by but he wasn't interested and kept walking.

I swallowed. She was a prostitute.

"I'm...my name is Jules," I said.

"Nicole," she said. We shook hands.

"How did you learn to speak English so well?"

"My clients," she said with a shrug. "Tourists from Aix and Nice."

"Oh," I said. "You're not from around here?"

"I am now. Four years. And you?"

"Five months."

"Were you on a cruise ship and couldn't get home?"

I wondered if she knew some tourists who that had happened to.

"Something like that," I said.

She looked around the market, her smile firmly in place.

"This probably isn't a good place for you to be," she said. "Are you lost?"

"I'm looking for someone. His name's Tristan Zabala. He has...he's..."

But Nicole was nodding and she'd lost her smile.

"I know him," she said, drawing a line down her mouth with her finger to indicate the hair lip. "A sad boy."

She narrowed her eyes at me. In the old days she might have wondered if I was an undercover police detective, but nowadays the police didn't have the resources for such things. And she knew it.

"Why do you search for him?" she asked warily.

I debated lying to her but in the end it was easier to tell the truth. I wasn't specifically trying to pin the murder on Tristan and even if I was, it was to help a sweet little old lady. Well, maybe not all that sweet...

"I think he might have seen a murder take place."

"*Vraiment?*" She was surprised and I thought it looked genuine. She didn't know about the murder. She seemed to be trying to work something out in her head and then she made up her mind and took me by the sleeve and pulled me into the curtained room.

There was a cot in there and a stack of stained sheets. Light from the opened top eliminated the need for candles or a lantern.

"Tristan lives further into the *Mégisseries*," she said.

"Does he live alone?"

She shook her head. "He lives with other young men who have no home."

Kind of like a post-apocalyptic French YMCA, I thought.

"Does he have any friends, do you know?" I asked.

"No. Except for...he has a friendship with an older man—one who shouldn't visit this side of town. But for Tristan's sake? I'm glad he does."

That was bizarre. *Tristan lives over here like the Artful Dodger?* And he has a relationship with an older man who *didn't* live here?

What would any sensible man want with someone like Tristan? I felt a cold shiver as I involuntarily entertained some possibilities.

"Can you describe the man?"

Nicole shook her head. "I don't want to get anyone in trouble. I think this man is being a good friend to Tristan."

Really.

The curtain parted and an astonishingly ugly old man poked his head through the opening and looked me up and down before breaking into a smile that looked like a broken picket fence that needed whitewashing. He fired off a bunch of what sounded like very lewd French but Nicole only laughed and pushed him away.

"*Attends*, Gilbert!" she said. "*Je viens en moment.*" Then she turned back to me. "You should go. It is not good for you here. You understand? Find Tristan when he visits his grandmother but do not come back. Okay?"

I nodded. I was a little shaken and while disappointed at the wasted trip, glad to get on my bike and head back toward safety.

"Thank you, Nicole," I said. "I'm glad I met you."

She smiled as she waved the old man over to her and ushered him into the tent.

"Me too, Jules," she said. "And tell Jim I said hello."

16

MURPHY'S LAW

It took the stupid mayor forever to leave.

Enora poured herself a large glass of whiskey and stood in the window of her hotel room looking out.

Thank God the policeman had opted to question her another day. She was sure she'd hidden her shaking hands from him but her voice was quite another thing. Even with that dingbat mayor saying how upset she was, Enora knew the policeman would interpret trembling hands as otherwise.

Not wanting to but not able to prevent herself, Enora closed her eyes and saw it again—just as she had been seeing it all day—the moment replayed in her head when she approached the éclair booth. It still amazed her that she'd had the courage to do something so lethal, so deadly, so...horrible.

Yes, she hated Lucien.

Had she meant to kill him?

Did that even matter now that he was dead?

It matters to the police.

She took a long swallow of the whiskey, grateful for its burn all the way down her throat.

She knew Lucien would eat the éclair. She knew all she had to do was hesitate and let him go first.

In a way it was like he killed himself!

And that's what she'd tell herself for as long as it took to ease out of this sickening guilt.

That's what she'd tell herself for as long as it took to finally believe it.

~

My mind was whirling as I pedaled back to the village. *Was Nicole telling me that she knew Jim?* What else could it mean? Okay, if that's true, so what? So she knew Jim. Did that mean…did it mean Jim goes out there? Was he getting… *serviced* at the black market?

That last thought nearly made me run into a shallow stone trench that bordered the road and it took fast reflexes to avoid ramming my bike into an old poster kiosk.

Well, honestly how well did I really know Jim? And if I looked at it honestly, was it the worst thing I'd ever heard?

Pretty revolting, I thought. *Going to a prostitute?*

On the other hand, what were his options? Jim and his girlfriend broke up four years ago and he'd been living alone all this time.

But still!

As I hit the last block before breaking free of Chabanel, I thought about riding by the police station to see if Madame C was feeling any more talkative but just the memory of her stubborn little face and her arms crossed on her chest made me reconsider.

I'd do better to continue trying to track down Tristan or

find any other clues that might lead to the real murderer. I slowed down when I approached a crossroad but without cars to worry about it was only ever pedestrians to look out for these days. Unfortunately for me, the one pedestrian I preferred not to see crossed right in front of me, forcing me to slam on the brakes of my bike.

Monsieur Gaillard, he of the pasture dalliance, stepped off the curb into the street in front of me. I know he did it on purpose because he gave me a smirk and held up his hand in a *stop* gesture.

The worst thing about seeing this jerk was the fact that he was walking with *Madame* Gaillard—my client. She was chatting away, oblivious of my presence since his bulk effectively blocked her view of me.

But it didn't block my view of his face and the message he was sending me.

Without proof, you have nothing.

I sighed. He wasn't wrong. With no concrete evidence I could hardly tell Madame Gaillard that her husband was cheating on her.

I waited for the couple to cross the street and disappear.

It was just as well. I'd been doing this private eye stuff for a few months and it totally wasn't working out. I hated to admit it because I'd argued long and hard with Luc about it and I didn't want him to know he was right.

Not only did I never get paid actual money—only live chickens and promises, which sounds like a better country western song than a career plan—but I only ever got cases that related to someone's disgusting, perverted actions. It was always a wayward husband or a thieving employee, never something noble or respectable like solving a cold case or proving some pillar of the community innocent of a crime.

"Jules! Wait up!"

I turned to see Katrine walking quickly toward me, a basket of produce on her arm. She reached me and we quickly air-kissed.

"Hey, Katrine. I didn't see you at the fair yesterday."

"Babette was sick," Katrine said. But she flushed when she said it and looked away.

That was odd. So was Babette really sick, I wondered? And if not, why was Katrine lying about it?

"I hope she's feeling better."

"It is nothing. But I heard about Madame C! It is terrible!"

"I know. Crazy old broad, confessing to murder. But you know her. There's no talking to her."

"She confessed?" Katrine's mouth dropped open.

"I thought you knew."

"No, I only heard that Madame Fournier claimed she saw Madame C ransacking Madame Zabala's booth."

So it was Madame Fournier who ratted Madame C out? I frowned. Did that make sense? I was sure the two of them weren't friends. But even if they were, Madame Fournier didn't strike me as the kind of person who'd play along with any of the Madame Twins' daft, delusional schemes.

So why would Madame Fournier say she saw Madame C in Madame Zabala's booth?

Unless she did.

But that can't be. Madame C was innocent.

Right?

"Jules? You okay?"

I shook myself out of my thoughts. "I'm just shocked that Madame Fournier would say that."

"The whole village is shocked," Katrine said. "But..." She shrugged.

"But what?"

"Well, it is not so terrible that Chef Chevalier...you know." She shrugged again.

I did know. It hadn't taken long for the whole village to hate on Chevalier. The first inclination of any village was always to distrust a stranger. And secondly, Chevalier acted the swine from his first steps in town.

No, it wasn't a surprise that nobody mourned him in Chabanel.

Katrine bustled off again with hand waves and promises of *let's get together soon* and I got back on my bike for the ride back to *La Fleurette*. As soon as I did, my mind was swamped once more with thoughts of how Jim knew Nicole and why Madame Fournier might lie about seeing Madame C.

Had Madame Fournier really seen her? Or was she protecting someone?

Come to that, I thought with a start, if the altercation in her bakery meant anything then Madame Fournier had a pretty big motive for wanting to see Lucien Chevalier writhing on the ground in mortal agony.

17

SINGLE LADIES

I got back to *La Fleurette* early afternoon. After a full afternoon of weeding the back garden, feeding the damn goats and helping Madame B preserve the last of the tomatoes and peppers, I was looking forward to an hour after my bath to just lose myself in a good book before Jim came over.

He typically came over most evenings—just as Luc used to do before our big break up. I know I shouldn't compare the two and usually I'm successful in not doing that or when I do I draw the lines firmly between American and French— not two men that I might view in a romantic light. Because as long as I put them into the two separate international camps, Jim and Luc came off as fairly equal and that was comfortable for me.

But as soon as I started looking at them as two men— two suitors—well, let's just say, I began to feel restless and uneasy.

I'm sure I don't at all know what that means. If Madame B and C spoke English better, I have no doubt they'd be able to explain it to me in no uncertain terms so here's me being grateful that their English is so bad.

Madame B came out of the kitchen where she'd been happily banging pots around for the last thirty minutes to stand in the doorway between the house and the back garden where I was seated, wrapped in a heavy wool throw trying to read my book. Cocoa was curled up at my feet but, as she does when anyone emerges from her favorite room in the house, she jerked her head up and looked expectantly at Madame B.

"*Ton ami, il est là,*" Madame B said briskly, informing me that Jim was on the front door step waiting to be allowed in.

I made a mental note to tell Jim to skip the front door from now on and just come around the house to the back entrance. Then glancing down at Cocoa I realized that wouldn't work. Cocoa had yet to grant *acceptable visitor* status to Jim. She probably picked that up from the Madame Twins but in any case, I'm pretty sure she'd view Jim as an invader if he tried to bypass the front door.

I got up from my chair to go to the front door.

"Do you need help with dinner?" I asked as I passed her. It was only a courtesy. I knew she wouldn't accept help with dinner while Jim was here.

Jim stood on the doorstep, holding two bottles of wine, a baguette and a box with a string wrapped around it that he must have gotten from Aix since Madame Fournier didn't bother with such elaborate packaging. Honestly, though, I could have told him—*should* have told him—that bringing pastries to *La Fleurette* was a bad move.

He did remember we'd just spent the last two weeks baking, hadn't he?

But I took the box and thanked him effusively and led him through the house and out to the back terrace. In case I haven't mentioned it, *La Fleurette* is a twelfth-century carriage house situated on a small rise surrounded by fields, and bordered on one side by a country road which separates us from a copse of trees.

The back garden is encased by an ancient stonewall that the cats are always leaping off of like it's some great adventure to explore the other side. There's a decrepit patio with more broken pavers than flat stones and a *potager* that the twins had recognized for what it was at first glance.

To me it had just looked like a tangle of weeds but once groomed and tended, it now provided—at least in summer —all the parsley, basil, peppers, dill and rosemary that we could ever want.

I led Jim through one of the two sets of French doors that opened up into the garden. Madame B was eating in the kitchen tonight claiming it was too cold outside, but I loved the chilly air. Once I put in a little fire in our outdoor fire pit—ignoring the disapproving glances from Madame B for wasting precious firewood—Jim and I would have a very cozy little supper under the leafless plane trees.

Once I settled him outside, I took the bread and wine into the kitchen and opened one bottle. I poured a glass for Madame B. She had her back to me at the stove but I knew she was aware of everything I did.

"Jim and I'll eat outside, Justine," I said brightly. I could see she'd already taken the *legumes farcis* out of the oven. The stuffed eggplant and peppers sat in a heavy casserole pan on top of the stove. The fragrance of the sausage and herbs she'd stuffed them with instantly made my mouth water.

I'd forgotten to pick up bread on my way back from town today and knew, as annoyed as Madame B might be at having Jim-not-Luc over for dinner, all would be mostly forgiven with the unexpected presence of the bread.

It was weird that Madame B and I hadn't spoken about Madame C all day. I got the idea that the subject wasn't welcome and since there really wasn't much to say, I didn't broach the topic. But Madame C's absence weighed heavily on both of us all afternoon.

I took the rest of the wine and two glasses back out to the patio where I saw that Jim was petting the Madame Twins' cat Camille. I was glad to see that since Cocoa was still watching him warily and my own cat—or at least the one I'd inherited from the people whose apartment I'd rented—was barely friendly to *me*, let alone strangers.

"Here you go," I said as I handed him a glass of wine.

The sun was in the process of setting and there was a beautiful illuminating glow that was backlighting Jim on the patio. I still hadn't decided what to say to him about what I'd discovered in *Mégisseries* so I decided, at least for now, not to mention that I'd been there at all.

"Have you heard the news?" Jim asked.

"There's news?" I frowned. Why was I always the last one to know what was going on in Chabanel? *Oh, yeah, that's right. Because I don't speak French.*

"The police released Madame Zabala last night."

"Well, that's not a surprise, I guess. After all, they've got a confessed murderer."

"Have you talked with Madame C today?"

"No," I said defensively. "What's the point? I know what she'll say." I began to mimic her voice. "*I am geel-tee of zees crime! You cannot tell me I am not!*"

Jim laughed ruefully.

"She is a stubborn one," he said. "They both are. Trust

me, I know the type. I have an old auntie back in Chicago who's just as obdurate."

I patted the outdoor chair next to mine and took a sip of my wine.

"You don't talk about your family much," I said.

He shrugged and sat down. "I guess I got in the habit of not sharing," he said. "Because of Sylvie."

I knew Sylvie was his mentally handicapped sister.

"You must miss her," I said.

Jim reached out and took my hand. "She died," he said.

"Oh, Jim, I'm sorry. I didn't know." Of course I didn't. He never talked about her.

"Aunt Ruth was really good with Sylvie. Much better than even my folks. But she was tough, you know? It was an odd combination. Honestly, it made me really appreciate strong women."

We sat quietly for a moment and I knew he was thinking of his sister. He didn't offer to tell me how Sylvie died and so I didn't ask. Everything in its own time.

"The last time I saw Sylvie," Jim said softly, "she asked me to bring her a picture of the Eiffel Tower. To her all of France was Paris, you know?"

I nodded.

"I sent her the picture and my mother told me Sylvie kept it pinned over her bed. She'd had someone write 'my brother lives here' underneath it. My mom took a photo of it and sent it to me."

I squeezed his hand and he looked at me as if a spell was broken. He smiled sadly.

Madame Becque came to the door and cleared her throat. Her subtle disdain was nearly as non-subtle as Madame C's.

"*Dîner*, Jules," she said before turning and leaving, Cocoa close at her heels.

Jim and I ate our dinner on the patio. The *legumes farcis* was delicious, of course. I'd only ever had stuffed peppers before the Madame Twins introduced me to the dish and now I'll never be able to go back to stuffed peppers.

I encouraged Jim to feed bits of bread to Cocoa—Madame C wasn't here to scowl at the misdemeanor—and was happy to see that the dog was open to being friends with him after that. I knew Madame B and C would be a little harder sell but they'd come around too, I felt sure.

After we finished eating and polished off the first bottle of wine, I was feeling very mellow and very attracted to this big American who—by the mere fact of being my countryman—knew me better than anyone else in this village could.

It's true we hadn't slept together *yet* but what with all the silent messages and eyebrow tweaks, I was pretty sure that was the next stage in our relationship.

"Katrine told me today that it was Madame Fournier who squealed on Madame C," I said.

Jim frowned. "She can only squeal if there's something to reveal. I thought you said Madame C couldn't possibly have done this."

I sat up straight in my chair and felt a pulse of excitement shoot through me.

"So that has to mean Madame Fournier lied, right?" I said.

"Or was mistaken."

"Mistaken to the point of making an accusation to the

police? I'm not buying it. She *lied*. I just have to find out why."

"Did you find Tristan?" Jim asked.

I chose my words carefully. First I hadn't really gotten any usable information from my visit—unless you count the tidbit that my boyfriend had possibly paid for sex at least once. And secondly I've learned the hard way that flimsy evidence combined with gut intuition does not tend to stack up as credible with most men. At least it wouldn't have with Luc.

"No. But I still intend to," I said.

"Do you know anything about the other chef?"

"Enora Roche? Do you think she saw the fair as an opportunity to kill her colleague?"

"I don't know. But she had opportunity. Maybe if you questioned her you'd find a motive."

"Maybe. I definitely got the impression she and Chevalier were more than just colleagues.

"Really?"

"It was obvious they were together."

Jim shook his head. "Not to me. Especially since she made a pass at me."

My mouth fell open.

"Surprised?" he said with a grin.

I recovered quickly. "That other women find you attractive? Not at all. I just picked up a different feel from her but I guess I was wrong. In any case, that certainly means she's a suspect. Who else?"

"What about Madame Fournier?"

"You mean because Chevalier publicly insulted her? I agree she had motive but probably no more than anyone else did. And certainly no more than Tristan did."

"Oh, that's right, you don't know, do you?

I hate it when people say stuff like that. It's like they're reveling in your ignorance and that's not very nice, is it?

"What are you talking about?"

"I ran into Theo Bardot," Jim said. "He told me Madame Fournier, Enola Roche and Lucien Chevalier all went to culinary school together."

18

BOAT ROCKING TIME

I couldn't believe what Jim had told me—the two chefs *knew* Madame Fournier from culinary school? They were all old friends?

That changed everything, but it didn't explain why Madame Fournier would try to point the finger at Madame C. After all, Enora Roche had already accused Madame Zabala.

Why would Madame Fournier implicate Madame C if they'd already arrested someone else for the crime? Wouldn't that just bring unwanted attention to her? If she *were* the killer, wouldn't she want to keep her head down?

"What do you think it all means?" I asked Jim.

He shrugged. "Maybe it's just an interesting fact and doesn't mean anything."

This is how I knew Jim would never make a good private investigator. The new information definitely meant *something*. I just didn't know what.

I wondered if Luc knew about this connection. Surely he'd interviewed Enora Roche by now. And since Madame

Fournier was their star witness, I could only assume he'd talked to her at length too.

If Luc didn't release Madame C by tomorrow—and by *release* I meant kick her out of the police station—I'd have to confront him with whatever game he thought he was playing. After all, I knew he didn't think Madame C did this. And if he really had released Madame Zabala he didn't think *she* did it either.

So who does he have in mind for it?

"Earth to Jules," Jim said tapping on my wrist. As soon as I broke out of my thoughts I registered that the temperature had dropped and the fire pit was only embers. I shivered and then smiled apologetically.

"Do you mind if we cut tonight short?" I said. "I'd like to have a one-on-one with Madame B before she gives me the excuse of being too sleepy."

"I'll agree on one condition," Jim said.

"And that is?"

"That you go on a picnic with me tomorrow evening. The weather's supposed to be nice and I'll bring everything we'll need."

Including a blanket, I'll wager. But I couldn't fault him for his suggestion. Spending time at *La Fleurette* wasn't as comfortable as it might be for any would-be suitors.

"That sounds lovely," I said.

His face broke into a grin of delight and I knew without a shadow of a doubt that he was thinking tomorrow was going to be *the night*. The night we advanced our relationship past just *seeing each other* into *knowing each other intimately*. I couldn't fault him for that either. But whether I was ready for that next step, I wasn't sure. I realized as I saw him stand up and prepare to leave that a part of me was hoping he'd offer up an explanation for how he knew Nicole.

Without my having to ask for it.

That was unfair. Asking men to read your mind is the biggest trap of all and I more than anyone knew that it never ends well.

Which, of course, will never stop me from doing it.

"Tomorrow then?" he said as he pulled me into his arms. He kept his hands on my waist but his kiss was deep and insistent. I liked the way he smelled and I liked the way he respected my hesitancy to move forward.

Yes, tomorrow was right. For both of us. It was time.

"Tomorrow," I said, kissing him back.

After Jim left, I collected our plates and cleaned them in the kitchen. I could see that Madame B had left the kitchen spotless with all the leftovers tucked away in the icebox—which was what I called the long-dead refrigerator. Amazingly, it still helped to put food in there. They didn't keep as long as a real refrigerator, of course, but it was better than nothing.

I let Neige out to join Camille who was waiting for her on the stonewall for their nightly hunt and went upstairs with Cocoa at my heels.

The lantern in Madame Becque's room was still on as I knew it would be.

"Hey, Justine," I said as I poked my head into her bedroom. Madame B's bedroom was as frilly and feminine as her sister's was spartan and cold. I'm not saying they had nothing in common in their personalities but yeah, you could say that. Cocoa shot out from behind me and jumped on the bed, turning in tight circles until she found just the right spot. As comfortable as she was making herself I knew she'd abandon her new nest as soon as she saw me leave the room.

Madame B was lying in bed, glasses on her nose, a large magnifying glass in one hand and a book in the other. She did not look at me with surprise but she was smiling—as per usual.

I sat on the edge of the bed. There was an ancient figurine on her side table of a girl with a goose in her arms. I wondered where Madame B got it and if she'd had it for most of her life. The two sisters had very few possessions—another mystery to be solved another day.

"Can I ask you a question?"

She closed her book and the smile stayed in place.

"Madame C confessed to the murder after Madame Zabala had been arrested," I said. "So did she do it to protect Madame Zabala?"

Madame B looked tired and for a minute I was pretty sure she wasn't going to answer me. But finally she did.

"Someone saw Léa in Agathe Zabala's booth," Madame B said.

"It was Marie Fournier who said that."

Madame B held out her hands as if to say, *and so*?

"It's just that—and bear with me here a moment—if Madame Zabala didn't kill the chef and Madame C didn't kill him—isn't what Madame C is doing right now wasting everyone's time and letting the real killer escape?"

Madame B just smiled enigmatically at me so I tried a different tack.

"You know, I've been looking for Madame Zabala's grandson for the past two days and I can't find him anywhere."

"Tristan Zabala did not kill the chef."

"Oh, really? You know that?"

She shrugged and opened her book back up.

"So let me get this straight. You don't want Madame Zabala going down for this and you don't want her grandson going down for it either."

She frowned. "Going down?"

"What if I told Luc that *I* did it?"

"*C'est ridicule.*"

"I had just as much access to Madame Zabala's booth while she was gone as Madame C. I think I'll tell him it was me."

"Stop! It was not you."

"It wasn't Madame C either so tell me why I shouldn't give a false confession. Tell me, Justine, or I'll go right down to the police station this minute and tell Luc it was me."

I have rarely seen Justine Becque agitated. She's usually the cool one. Well, warm and fuzzy but also cool.

"I will tell you," she said finally. "But Léa will not retract her confession."

"Fine. Just tell me why."

"My sister will be very angry with me."

"Lucky for you then that she'll be in prison for life. Let's hear it."

She gave me a chastising glance and then her face became etched in pain. I reminded myself that in her mind she was breaking a confidence.

"Agathe and I were not friends before the war," she said. "Her family was wealthy and she and my sister and I did not…"

I wanted to jump in and suggest fraternize but bit my lip harder. As it was she was telling the story in a mixture of English and French and I was really only understanding every fourth word or so.

Fortunately, it was enough.

"Agathe's mother died years ago," Justine continued. "Her brother was a prisoner of war in Germany. Her father was a weak man but he adored his daughter. *Elle était belle.*" *She was beautiful.*

Justine shrugged as if allowing the compliment reluctantly.

"We were occupied in Chabanel—as in all of Provence. The Germans came and took ...everything—the best food, all of the wine, our livestock."

I could see that Justine was remembering that time and I felt a sudden impulse to tell her *never mind*, I didn't want to know. Every once in a while the sisters would tell stories of the war but usually only ones that were amusing or not serious. I was suddenly sorry I was putting her through this.

"Agathe's father would not allow her to join *l'resistance*. He feared losing her like her brother. So she became close to the Germans to get *l'information*. To one German in particular."

Uh-oh. I did not like where this was going.

"He was an officer. She got information from him that she passed on to our side. And that helped our cause."

So yay, Agathe, I thought, waiting for the other shoe to drop.

"Once the Germans are leaving Provence we are seeing that Agathe is with child," Justine said with a long sigh. "All of our young men were gone. It could only be the German officer."

Madame B carefully eased out the creases in the sheet on her bed. Her hands were shaking.

"Agathe was accused of being a collaborator," she said.

I felt myself flushing with anger. After everything she'd done? The village turned on her? What bitch turned her in? Because make no mistake it was a woman.

"At her trial when asked if Agathe Zabala deserved to be ...punished for her crimes...." A tear streaked down Justine's face and fell on the sheet. She took in a long breath.

"Léa came forward," Justine said quietly. "She accused Agathe of fraternizing with the enemy." She looked at me, her lips trembling. "It was the truth."

"But not the whole truth," I said.

"Agathe was taken to the *place de maire* where she was... publicly shamed. To this day she wears her hair long to hide the scars on her neck where the hot tar peeled her skin away."

I felt sick and the backs of my hands prickled uncomfortably as if I could feel the tar myself.

"Why?" I said. "Why did Léa do it? She knew the truth. She knew Agathe was a patriot."

"It is shameful," Justine said in a low voice.

"Tell me."

She took in another long breath as if for strength.

"Léa caught her fiancé—Thierry Cazaly—in Agathe's arms. It was months before the occupation. Léa forgave him."

"But Léa never forgave Madame Zabala."

"No."

I felt a heavy feeling in my stomach.

Madame C thinks by sacrificing herself for Madame Zabala, she'll be able to even the balance sheet.

"But what if Madame Zabala *didn't* kill the chef?"

Justine shrugged. "It is enough that people think she did."

"Even if it means the real killer gets away?"

"We do not know she is not the killer or as you have said, her great-grandson."

"So Léa would sacrifice herself for Tristan too?"

Madame B shrugged but nodded.

I was ten seconds from saying how totally random and crazy all of this was when I noticed Cocoa was no longer on the bed. I'd been so entranced in the story I didn't see the moment she left. It was unusual for her to be anywhere I wasn't. I stood up and looked around the room.

Out of the corner of my eye, I caught a glimpse of the dog in the hallway. She was watching me and whining—something else I hadn't noticed until Justine's story was done.

Just as I was about to go into the hall to find out why she was acting so odd, I stopped suddenly.

I smelled smoke.

19

THE BITE IS MARGINALLY WORSE

The hall began to fill with smoke as I flung back the covers on Justine's bed and grabbed her arm.

"The house is on fire!" I said, tossing her the slippers that were on the floor by her bed. "We need to get out."

At first Justine didn't move, just stared at me and the doorway to the hall which was quickly filling with smoke. Cocoa had retreated into the bedroom.

I didn't know where the fire was but I knew the hall was quickly becoming impassable. I ran to Justine's bedroom window, which looked out over the back garden. The tile roof that jutted out over the French doors in back presented a sharp drop off but it was better than nothing. I knew we had to get out this window and into the garden.

Just before I turned to grab bedding to help soften our jump to the terrace below, I saw movement in the field beyond the stone wall that enclosed our garden.

It wasn't a full moon but it was light enough to clearly see the figure running away from the house.

~

Luc had just passed the darkened post office when old Monsieur Augustin came riding up on his donkey. The sight of him was ludicrous and would have made Luc laugh if it weren't for the fact that it could only mean something terrible had happened.

Monsieur Augustin shouted, "Fire at *La Fleurette!* Hurry!"

Luc's first impulse was to run straight to *La Fleurette*. With a fire, every second counted. But he also knew if there were injuries, he would need the car to drive immediately to the Aix hospital.

He agonized as he turned away from the direction of *La Fleurette* and ran back to the station, his heart bursting out of his chest.

The sounds of his shoes against the ancient cobblestones sounded like gunfire in his ears.

~

There were enough bedclothes in the garden to keep all of us warm into the night should that be necessary. The fire itself seemed to be limited to one section of the house—the jetty—a portion on the upper story of the house which was mostly wood. In fact it was the only part of the old farmhouse that was not made of stone.

I knew my hair smelled like smoke and that my face and arms were streaked with soot. I'd tied a sheet around Justine's waist and by leveraging the sheet around one post of Justine's bed was able to lower her to the garden and then did the same with Cocoa although she fought gallantly not to leave me.

By the time it was my turn, I could barely breathe. The smoke had breeched Justine's room and my eyes stung and wept. I grabbed the sheet tied to the bedpost, snatched up the little ceramic figurine from Justine's night stand, and crawled down the sheet until my feet hit the pavers below.

Justine and I walked to the far edge of the garden and watched the fire as flames leapt and danced around the jetty. Cocoa pressed herself tightly against the front of my legs and we all leaned against the stone wall. Both cats sat on the wall and watched the fire as if they'd paid for the show and expected their money's worth.

As soon as I had a moment to breathe, count heads and realize we were safe, I also had a moment to remember the figure I saw running away. It could have been a woman. Or a teen.

Tristan.

Justine said nothing as we watched the flames destroy the top of the jetty. We'd both heard the fire alarm bell ringing from town. It sounded very far away and I had no idea how long it would take to get them to the house. I knelt and put an arm around Cocoa who continued to shiver.

I didn't hear the car drive up but, separated from the front of the house and with the low roar and crackle of the fire, it was no wonder.

I saw Luc though. He crashed through the garden gate at a dead run until he saw us and then ran across the terrace to us—never once tripping in the dark. I saw his eyes go first to Justine, assess her, and then to me. I stood up just in time to feel his arms go around me and pull me into his chest, his face buried in my hair.

It was just a moment and only a moment. Before I even knew what had happened, he'd released me and turned to face the burning house. As we watched, the gabled top of the jetty crumbled and broke apart, falling to the terrace in a shower of sparks.

"Whoever did this was an idiot," Luc said, watching the now dying fire. "*La Fleurette* is almost completely stone."

"I saw him," I said. "Or her. Running away."

I pointed over the stone wall. The field behind us did not lead to Chabanel. Whoever did this either didn't return directly to the village, hadn't originally come from the village, or was lost.

"Stay here," Luc said and left to greet the horse-drawn fire truck at the front of the house.

I wanted to tell him to forget it. To tell the volunteer fire men to keep their water for someone with a wooden house who'd really need it some day. Luc was right. *La Fleurette* was almost all stone. So was the person who did this really an idiot? Or was this a warning?

Justine wrapped her duvet around her shoulders and went to the French doors that led into the house. She opened the doors but no clouds of smoke billowed out. The jetty had been adjacent to the bedrooms so it stood to reason that the hallway would be affected upstairs. It didn't look like the kitchen or the downstairs had been touched at all.

I knew Justine would not be able to endure having people in her house without offering them refreshments.

Not even people with stretchers and fire hoses.

Although better, Cocoa was still trembling and I had to admit I preferred to be out in the evening air. I could see Madame B through the window of the kitchen as she lit the stove to make coffee for the men. She'd probably put together a plate of sandwiches while she was at it. I shook my head in amazement.

As I stood there, enjoying the firm solidity of the wall to

my back and the crisp night air, I thought about the story that Justine had told me tonight. It wasn't like I ever doubted Madame C's innocence. I knew she hadn't killed the chef.

But now I knew why she needed to do this.

As I reflected on what I could do with this new information, Luc came out of the house.

Will I ever stop enjoying how damn sexy he looks? Even as mad as I am at him —and trust me I still am—I can't help enjoying how he carries himself, the tilt of his head, the way he walks into any situation and knows exactly what to do.

And I also can't help remembering the feel of his arms around me just moments before.

"You said you saw someone?" he said without preamble.

"Running away. From the bedroom window."

"Your bedroom window faces the front."

Now that's interesting. How did he know which way my bedroom faces?

"I was with Madame B in her bedroom."

He nodded and glanced back at the house.

"Who was here tonight?

"Just me, Jim and Madame B."

"Jim Anderson?"

It's not often you can catch Luc where he's not in complete control of what he's doing or saying. Something about knowing that made me just want to mess him up a little—especially when I saw him flinch at the mention of Jim's name.

"We're seeing each other, you see," I said nonchalantly, enjoying the look of displeasure that was developing in his face. "That's how it's done where I come from. You spend time together and then you..."

One thing I can tell you about that moment is that I had no idea he was going to kiss me.

None.

The second his lips were on mine—so firm, so demanding—I felt myself just melt into him. And then a powerful warmth ignited in me—toes to fingertips—and I kissed him back.

And then remembered who he was.

I pulled away. "How dare you!" I gasped, stepping away from him in case he had some sort of magical pull that proximity made me helpless to withstand.

"You kissed me back," he said with a smile.

"I most certainly did not! You have overstepped yourself!"

"This isn't an episode of Downton Abbey, *chérie*," Luc said, laughing. "And now I know you're not sleeping with Anderson."

"Don't call me that and how dare...yes, of course we are! Every night if you must know."

I wanted so much to slap that smug, happy look from his face. The face that knew me, knew the truth. The face that could kiss me so I wanted to just vibrate with the pleasure of it.

Why didn't Jim's kisses do this?

"You haven't done it with him yet," he said.

"That is none of your business!" I huffed, turning to stalk back into the house and nearly tripping over Cocoa in the process, effectively turning my big dramatic exit into a vaudeville skit.

~

Madame Fournier felt the excitement of what she was about to do spread from the tight grip she had on her purse up her legs and into her chest. She had thought about it all day. She knew she was through thinking.

She had set this whole thing in motion and she couldn't stop now. Everything would have been for nothing if she stopped now. From where she stood in the shadow of the alley that faced the hotel, she could easily pick out Enora Roche's window. It was the only one with a lantern burning.

In the window.

Beckoning.

Calling me to finish it, Marie thought, her mind whirling with emotion. It was time. Finally.

She left the alley but kept to the shadows, moving quickly across the street to the hotel. Just around the back was the fire escape ladder. It would take her to the hall on Enora's floor.

I will be in and out and no one the wiser, she thought. The thrill of finally doing it—finishing it—infused her as every step took her closer to the hotel.

To the end of her fight with her demon.

20

BELOW THE BELT

The next morning Luc woke to a beautiful fall day. The air was cold but bright, the sun warm everywhere it touched and the colors of Provence popped like a Cezanne painting.

Ever since the EMP Luc had moved into a spare room at the *police municipale*. With the near constant plethora of complaints—both trivial and real—coming from the villagers since the EMP he'd been spending most of his waking moments at the station anyway. With no family and most of his meals eaten at the Café Sucre or out of paper bag, it just made sense.

Plus, he liked being the first one in the office every morning.

He made coffee and went immediately to check on Madame C. Eloise would bring croissants with her when she arrived.

This morning, Luc felt a lightness in his arms and legs. He felt good—damn good! It was pretty clear that Jules was just a few kisses away from forgiving him and on top of that

Tristan Zabala was spied by no fewer than two neighbors sneaking away from *La Fleurette* last night.

All in all, a great morning.

Luc would send Matteo out as soon as the detective showed up for work to arrest Tristan on suspicion of arson.

"Good morning, Madame Cazaly," Luc said as he knocked on his office door and entered with the coffee.

He shouldn't have been surprised to see she was already dressed. She wore head to foot black—had done for as long as Luc could remember. She sat at his desk, her ankles crossed, her hands in her lap. The single bed in the room had been made.

"Good morning, Chief DeBray," Madame C said primly, taking the coffee not unlike how Luc imagined the Queen herself might accept it.

"Jules will be here in a minute to take you home," Luc said. He'd arranged it with Jules last night.

"If you think that's best." Madame C sipped her coffee. Luc knew the coffee wasn't great but to her credit she didn't make a face.

"I'm going to trust you not to skip town," he said with a smile.

She raised an eyebrow at him. "I know you're not taking me seriously, Chief. But that is quite rude."

"I apologize, Madame Cazaly."

The sound of the front door opening made them both turn in that direction.

"That would be the sound of your croissants arriving, I believe," Luc said as he left the room to walk down the hall. Both Matteo and Eloise came in together. Behind them was a man Luc recognized as Monsieur Bonnet, the concierge at the village hotel.

"Chief," Eloise said dropping the bag of pastries on the

front desk and wriggling out of her coat. "Monsieur Bonnet is here to say something has happened at the hotel."

~

That morning when I came to get Madame C I was wondering if I'd run into Luc but Eloise said something was going on at the Chabanel hotel that he had to go deal with.

Madame C was remarkably closed-mouthed on the walk back to *La Fleurette*. Not that I expected any different. She was closed-mouthed at the best of times. As we walked, I couldn't help but envision her as the young and beautiful Léa during the war—incensed and jealous by the even more beautiful Agathe Zabala—to the point where she was driven to commit a terrible act.

We all make mistakes. But so far I have to say none of the boners I've made have resulted in any of my friends being dipped in hot tar.

I knew I wasn't being fair. I can't even imagine how war changes people. I'm sure both Léa and Justine were sweet young girls with dreams of marriage and making families until the Nazis came with their reprisals and tortures. It was unimaginable and whoever those girls had been before the war, well, they were nowhere to be found after.

It was something I just couldn't fathom.

Something else I couldn't fathom was whatever it was that had happened last night with Luc.

I still couldn't believe we'd kissed. He'd *kissed* me. I might even have kissed him back.

Our first kiss.

As soon as I thought of it that way I blushed angrily. A first kiss suggests there would be more and there would so not be more between me and Luc.

Who does he think he is? Does he think he can keep me a prisoner here in France, dictate who I see and don't see and then kiss me whenever he wants?

And I was vulnerable last night! I was outside in my bare feet watching my house on fire!

I shook away my pique and chased all thoughts of Luc—*and that kiss*—from my mind. *Keep your eye on the main thing*, I scolded myself. And the main thing right now was attempting to keep Madame C from going to prison for a crime she didn't commit.

After delivering the unrepentant jailbird to her sister—and witnessing the shortest hug on record between them—the two sisters immediately set out to clean up the smoke damage that had scorched the upper tympanum over the kitchen door on the back of the house.

I'm sure my help would have been welcome but honestly, I had a murderer to find.

And oh yeah, a picnic to get out of.

Not that I wanted to dump Jim. I most certainly did not. But last night with Luc was discombobulating on a lot of different levels. I couldn't help ask myself why I didn't feel the same way when Jim took me in his arms. And you know? I've found that those are the questions you need to pay attention to.

I was just thinking of slowing things down. It was pretty clear that Jim had high hopes for this picnic. Hopes that involved bringing us to the "next level."

And one thing I knew after being kissed by Luc DeBray last night: I wasn't ready for that next level. At least not with Jim Anderson.

Since I was having difficulty tracking down the elusive Tristan, I thought a visit to the local *boulangerie* might be a logical next step for me. At the very least I'd find out if Luc had questioned Madame Fournier.

When I arrived at the *boulangerie* it had started to rain again. I saw that there were workmen at the bakery positioning a brand new window where the boards were. The new pane of glass didn't have all the fancy writing on it that the first one did but that would just make it easier to view all the goodies in the bakery window.

I parked my bike and watched from across the street for a moment. I could see why they'd chosen midmorning to do the job. The big rush at the bakery was typically early morning and then again during teatime or *un gouter* as the French call it around four o'clock, and then lastly right around dinner time.

There was one woman at the counter inside. When I saw her turn and head out, I went in. Madame Fournier had always been as friendly to me as she has anyone else, that is to say, not very. But I knew the moment she saw me she'd be on guard. After all, she was the one who'd pointed the finger at Madame C. It stood to reason she'd expect I'd have a bone to pick with her.

"*Bonjour*, Madame Fournier," I said as I approached the display case.

"*Bonjour*, Madame," she said tightly, her eyes watching me, her manner nervous and fidgety.

I didn't remember her English being particularly good but as I didn't have a translator and my own French was without doubt worse, I just took the plunge. I didn't want to dilly-dally and end up with a line of nosy villagers behind me waiting to buy their daily baguettes while I interrogated her.

"Why did you say you saw Madame C in Madame Zabala's booth?"

She flushed red—not in an ashamed or confessionary way— but in anger, and spouted off a bunch of French that I didn't get. I *did* get that she wasn't denying making the accusation. Amazingly, I didn't need to understand her words to understand her.

"*Voulez-vous acheter quelque chose*, Madame?" she said tartly, clearly ready to toss me out unless I bought something.

If I thought Madame Fournier was acting a little edgy *before* I asked my question, she was definitely ready to go off like a rocket now. Nonetheless. I decided to go for it.

"So I hear you knew both chefs personally? You all went to culinary school together?"

At first she stared at me like she didn't understand me and I was about to search for better words—or to drop in a few French ones if that might help—when she lunged across the counter at me. I only had a second's warning before I jerked backward where she couldn't reach me.

"*Allez! Allez!*" she screamed. The rest of what she screamed I did not understand, but I did understand that she was wrestling with the hook on the underside of her counter to push open the piece that would let her break free of her confines.

I didn't think *that* was in anyone's best interests and so I bolted out of the shop, tripped and put a foot right into the new plane of glass the workmen had laid aside.

21

WHAT'S LOVE GOT TO DO WITH IT?

I must say I felt terrible about the broken glass but not enough to stop and talk about it and besides there was an argument to be made that Madame Fournier shouldn't have attempted to chase me out of her store. I take complete responsibility for the glass. I do. And if I hadn't been in immediate fear of damage to life and limb, I would have stopped to assure Madame Fournier of exactly that.

Except she probably wouldn't have understood me.

Anyway, instead I jumped on my bike in a mad hurry and headed down the block in the now pouring rain at triple speed.

I was obviously going to have to chalk this morning's work up in the loss column. I'd found out nothing except that Madame Fournier was excitable and knew more English than I thought.

As I rode down the bumpy cobblestone street, I decided to head toward Jim's place. Now that it was raining, even if it quit within the hour, the grass would be too wet for anybody to have a picnic. Mother Nature had just bought me a reprieve.

Once on his street, I pushed open the main door that led to Jim's courtyard where I left my bike. I knocked loudly on his front door but there was no answer. That bothered me a little. Not that he should be at home waiting for me to come by unannounced but I was sure he must have heard about the fire at *La Fleurette*. It wasn't like him not to come check on me. I scribbled a quick note suggesting a rain check for our picnic and stuck it onto his door with one of the many thumbtacks that were there for that reason.

I collected my bike and tried to collect my thoughts too.

Who else was there to talk to? Maybe Eloise? She was always good for releasing information she shouldn't about any open cases Luc was working on. I hated taking advantage of her gullibility but these are the things we private investigators are forced to do in order to get to the truth.

Yeah, when I heard it in my head it didn't sound believable to me either.

I was about to get back on my bike when I recognized a familiar figure ahead of me on the street. The bulky form of none other than Agathe Zabala.

∽

I caught up with Madame Zabala and immediately pantomimed the suggestion of sitting and having a cup of coffee somewhere out of the rain but she shook her head. I don't know if it was because she associated me with Madame C or she just wanted to be alone but she didn't even break stride as I walked next to her.

Her French was a little easier to understand than most and I wasn't sure if that was the accent or because she was using simple vocabulary. Whatever it was, I was grateful.

"I'm so glad they let you and Madame Cazaly go free," I

said, quickly running out of breath trying to keep up with her.

"They arrest my grandson," she said brusquely in French.

"They've arrested Tristan?" A part of me was thinking *it's about time*, but another part of me was truly surprised. Had there been new evidence?

"I'm sorry to hear that," I said, not really knowing what one says in a situation like this but not wanting to be a jerk about it.

"He was not raised with men. You see that?"

Okay so I'm sure I didn't understand that sentence at all. It made no sense. But I smiled and hoped there'd be more to come that would make it clearer.

The rain was falling on us and while like most self-respecting old ladies, Madame Zabala had an umbrella that was keeping her dry, me, not so much. But there was something about the rain and the fact that we weren't directly looking at each other that was allowing Madame Zabala to speak more freely. I don't know what it was but I had a strong sense there was no way she'd be this honest with me if we were looking at each other nice and dry across a café table.

"Perhaps he is drawn to older men, yes? Not unnaturally you understand." She gave me a quick look—the first since I'd started walking with her. "But as a boy looks to his father."

Okay so now I *really* had no idea what she was talking about.

Did she mean Tristan didn't have a father so he looked up to other men? Why was she telling me this? Had Tristan confessed to the murder? Maybe Luc—as the older man—had gotten him to confess?

While I was trying to sort all this out in my mind, Madame Zabala turned down an alley and disappeared just like that. No goodbyes or *oh this is my street*.

Just gone.

I shivered in the now stronger downpour and hopped on my bike in search of an overhang to wait out the worst of the rain.

As I rode I realized that what Madame Zabala had said —as conflated and baffling as it was—made me think about what Nicole had said about Tristan seeming to gravitate toward a man old enough to be his father. Not in a sexual way, Nicole had stressed.

But it made me think.

On the one hand, if Luc really did get Tristan to confess then we were done here and I could go find some unhappy villager in need of my services to track down their wayward cheating spouse.

But just to dot the last *i* and cross the last *t* after what Madame Zabala had revealed, I couldn't help but feel a strong urge to go back to *Mégisseries* to ask Nicole a few more questions…just to fill in some of the blanks.

∽

The market looked a lot seedier at this time of day—which was just before sundown. Because it had been raining on and off all day I didn't realize it was as late as it was when I set out but I wasn't sure it really mattered. I had one errand to do and it shouldn't take long.

I should be able to find Nicole—after all I had a pretty good idea of where she was—ask my questions and be back on my bike in less then thirty minutes.

That was the plan.

As I pedaled to the end of the market, past all the closed kiosks, I could see Nicole standing out in front of her little curtained booth, holding a pink *Hello Kitty* umbrella. It made me pause for a minute and think that Nicole was probably younger than I'd originally thought.

She saw me coming and smiled as I skidded to a stop in front of her.

"You shouldn't be here," she said. But her smile said otherwise. I don't know who Nicole's friends were on the dodgy side of the tracks but for whatever reason, she was happy to see me.

"I have a quick question for you," I said, the rain flattening my hair and turning the collar of my favorite Dolce & Gabbana blouse under my jacket into a wilted, soggy rag.

"Want to come inside?" She was already closing up her umbrella.

I joined her inside the tent. The mugginess of the rain didn't do wonderful things to the air in the tent and there was a definite pong I didn't want to attempt to identify. But when I saw Nicole shake the rain off her little pink umbrella, I felt sorry that I hadn't brought her a gift of some kind.

"You came back to ask me about Jim," Nicole said settling on the little cot.

As a matter of fact I did want to ask her about that, even if it hadn't been at the top of my list.

"Now that you mention it," I said.

She shrugged. "It was nothing. We only talked."

"Can I ask the last time you…talked…with him?"

She wrinkled her nose and squinted at me as if trying to figure me out.

"He was lonely," Nicole said, smiling at me in what I'm sure she thought was a reassuring gesture.

To me, it looked pitying.

"How long ago?" I asked again.

"A year? Perhaps more."

I took a deep breath. Whatever happened to me and Jim —and for whatever reason—it wouldn't be because he was lonely at some point in his life and paid for sex—if that's what happened.

But he still needs to mention it to me.

"I wanted to ask you about the older man you said hangs out with Tristan," I said. "It just sounds odd to me that an older man—one who doesn't belong here— would do that."

"He is, how you are saying? like an uncle."

"If you say so. But why? What is this so-called *uncle* getting out of befriending someone like Tristan?"

"Someone like Tristan?" I could see Nicole's eyes harden and I knew I was suddenly on shaky ground.

"I meant someone young and confused," I said. "Someone deformed and angry about it. Why is this older man with him?"

"He wants to help Tristan."

"What do they *do* together?"

Nicole pointed to a street visible through the rain at the end of the market. "There's a bar down there. They drink beer."

I glanced in the direction she pointed. "Okay. Can you give me a name?"

"I don't know his name."

"Can you describe him?"

"Why should I?"

"I can pay you."

"How much?"

"Look, I want what's best for Tristan too, you know." That is a foul lie and one I'm sure she can see on my face.

"Ten euros?"

I did not have ten euros. God, did *anyone* have ten euros these days? I rubbed my hands against my wet jeans in mild frustration.

"How about five?" I said, hoping I could manage that.

"When?"

"The weekend. But I need to know the description of the guy now."

At first I didn't think she'd tell me. And I honestly couldn't say why I thought this older man's identity was so important except for the fact that I just couldn't understand why anyone *normal* would befriend someone like Tristan. Something told me this older man—whoever he was—was the missing link.

"I believe he is trying to help Tristan," Nicole said.

"So you said. Tall? Fat? Does he have a beard?"

She sighed. "Heavy. Not tall. Square face, little piggy eyes."

My mind raced to try to put these descriptors into my memory bank of faces in Chabanel. I looked at her helplessly, hoping she had more to give me.

"He wears a uniform," she said, looking down at her hands.

"What kind of uniform?" I said, feeling my heart start to race.

"A policeman's uniform."

22

CLOSING RANKS

Jim walked the perimeter of the little *boulangerie*, a wicker basket on his arm and a definite bounce in his step. He'd already hit the cheese shop and the produce market this morning. Now he needed bread but also something sweet. Petit-fours would be good.

Tonight's picnic had to be perfect.

He could already tell that Jules was a little hesitant to take their relationship to the next level. And that was fine. He was happy to wait.

Well, maybe *happy* wasn't the right word.

But to be with Jules? To know that she'd chosen him? He'd wait as long as it took.

"Monsieur Anderson?"

Jim looked at Madame Fournier, the proprietor. She held out a sample of a *mille-feuille*. Jim smiled and accepted the sample. For a simple village bakery, Madame Fournier was really a master at the more delicate pastries. He was surprised she hadn't entered the pastry contest herself.

Probably didn't want to show up all the village ladies.

The *mille-feuille* was light and sweet and dissolved on his tongue.

"*C'est bon*, Madame Fournier," he said. "*Je vais le prendre*,"

"*Merci*," she said. "*Combien*?"

"*Six*."

She nodded and began wrapping up his pastries with the bread he'd already picked out.

There were several other shoppers in the bakery. It was still raining so presumably at least some of them were loitering to avoid going out in it. Jim knew there was a good chance he and Jules would have to push the picnic off to another night. That was all right. Everything except the baguette would keep and he'd just run by here and pick up another one tomorrow.

"A special event, Monsieur?" one of the ladies asked him.

"You could say that," Jim said, unable to hide a grin. "A romantic picnic with my girlfriend."

"Oh, very nice, Monsieur. You are going to *the quarry*? That is particularly beautiful around here."

"*Non*, do not tell him that!" another woman said. "They should go to *la petit gorge*." She was an elderly woman and looked earnestly at Jim. "It is not far at all. Barely three miles from Chabanel. Will you ride your bikes?"

"Walk, I think," Jim said, feeling a little embarrassed by the sudden attention from the ladies.

"The ground will be too wet for a picnic today," the first woman said.

Madame Fournier cleared her throat to indicate his purchases were ready.

"Well, we will do it tomorrow then," Jim said. "We are in no hurry."

"That is the very best way to approach love," one of the

old women said and the rest of the shoppers giggled or chortled at Jim's expense.

He grinned good-naturedly and took his purchases outside, flipping up his collar against the rain.

He ran through his mental shopping list: wine, bread, cheese, pastries, olives. As he stood in front of the bakery he caught a glimpse of Luc DeBray driving past in the ancient Cv2 he used as a police vehicle.

Seeing DeBray made Jim think of one more thing he might do to make this evening absolutely perfect.

∼

Holy crap.

Adrien *Matteo* was friends with Tristan? Did that make any sense at all? Was he undercover? But no, Nicole said he was in his police uniform.

Why would Matteo befriend Tristan? Doesn't he arrest him on a regular basis? Are they *friends*?

The thought of Matteo having a beer with Tristan just wouldn't make sense in my brain. Matteo was so by-the-book, so officious. Him reaching out to Tristan to do anything but cuff him around the ears was an image that wouldn't gel.

But why would Nicole lie about it?

Was there anyone else in a police uniform who was fat with beady eyes?

It had to be Matteo.

I ground my teeth just thinking about it.

I *knew* there was something squirrelly about that guy! Whatever he was doing in *Mégisseries*—and especially whatever he was doing with Tristan—was definitely not on the up and up. I was sure Luc didn't know about this.

I rode my bike back to Chabanel in the gloom of the coming evening, my thoughts focused on what Nicole had told me and what it could possibly mean when I saw the distinct figure of Sergeant Eloise Basile ahead of me. She was wearing a raincoat and carrying a lunch pail so I figured she was done for the day and headed home.

Perfect! A little after-work drink to loosen up her tongue and maybe I'll finally get some information about this damn case that I can actually use!

"Hey, Eloise," I said as I was gliding to a stop next to her. "Haven't seen you in awhile."

"Hello, Jules," she said warily. Luc had probably warned her about talking to me. He does that a lot. But he doesn't know the power of sisterhood.

"You're working long hours these days," I said casually. "Any leads on the Chevalier murder?"

"I'm not supposed to talk to you."

"Well, that's just silly. Let me buy you a drink."

I knew Eloise lived alone and that she didn't date anyone in Chabanel—or outside Chabanel come to think of it. She was young and hopeful that her time at the *police municipale* would advance her career. But she was also lonely. Anyone could see that.

"You know," I said, "Café Sucre has the best *bourride*. Aren't you hungry after a long day?"

"I really am," Eloise said wistfully, glancing in the direction of the street that would take us to Café Sucre.

Once I parked my bike and we settled in at a table at the café I ordered the popular fish soup for both of us. It wasn't raining any more but it was full-on dark. The Madame Twins would probably be wondering where I was but I was fairly confident they wouldn't send out a search party.

Fairly.

"It's great having Madame C home again," I said, after Theo took our meal order.

Eloise looked at me with surprise and I realized I'd misspoken.

Was it really believable that it was great having that old crosspatch home? *Now Eloise knows I'm up to something.*

But it turns out, no!

"We all love Madame C," Eloise said. "And I can't tell you how excited we were to find the culprit who'd tried to burn *La Fleurette*."

"Really? When did that happen? Who was it?"

"Matteo went out this afternoon and arrested Tristan Zabala on suspicion of arson," Eloise said, her eyes focused only on the creamy white fish soup as Theo set the bowl in front of her.

Well, if anyone could find Tristan I guess Matteo could, I thought.

"How did the police know it was Tristan?" I asked.

"Two of your neighbors reported seeing him running away last night."

Thank God for nosy neighbors.

"So you aren't looking at him for Chevalier's murder?"

Eloise brought her soup spoon to her mouth and our eyes met.

"I don't know about that," she said and popped the spoon into her mouth. "Luc is in charge of the case."

I gave Eloise a moment to take a healthy swig of her wine before pressing further.

"Any word back yet on what kind of poison it was in the éclair?"

"The lab said it was digitalis. It's found in foxglove which is very easy to grow. It has a strong odor. Luc thinks maybe the killer only wanted to warn Chevalier and assumed he'd smell the odor and refuse to eat it."

"Good point. So if it had a foul odor why would Chevalier bite into the éclair?"

"He had a bad cold. He probably couldn't smell it."

Interesting.

"You know," I said, "I was watching the two judges make the rounds that day and I know my testimony might not be..."

"Credible," Eloise finished. "Because you live with the prime suspect."

"Yeah. Okay. So take it for what it's worth but what I saw was the two judges *taking turns* as they judged the various pastries."

"So?"

"Well, unless I'm wrong and I'm not, it was Enora Roche's turn to sample from Madame Zabala's pastry booth."

Eloise's eyes became large. "Are you sure?"

Honestly, while I was *fairly* sure, I had to admit, I wasn't positive.

"Absolutely sure," I said. "So if it's true that Roche was to have taken the first bite, why did Chevalier end up eating the éclair instead? It was like Roche knew the éclair was poisoned."

"You think Enora Roche killed Lucien Chevalier? Why would she?"

"Well, that would be one of the things you might want to find out. Were they lovers? I saw them holding hands but I also saw them argue."

"Lovers argue."

"Of course they do. I'm just saying you should check it out."

"So you think Enora Roche killed her colleague?"

"I think it's something to consider," I said, sipping my wine and feeling satisfied that I'd effectively deflected some attention away from Madame C and her confession.

"Under normal circumstances I think Luc would consider it," Eloise said with a sigh. "I'd much rather a stranger be responsible for this crime than one of our own."

"Well, then…"

"Except how do you explain the big bag of foxglove we found in Madame C's booth at the fair?"

∼

Luc stared at the recent report back from the lab in Nice. It was definitely digitalis that killed Chevalier. Not only had the éclair found on the ground by the body been injected with a boiled-down concoction of the foxglove leaves, but there had been enough to kill ten men in the one bite of éclair that was found in Chevalier's stomach.

Who had done this? And why did they want to make it look as if Madame C had?

"Chief?"

Luc looked up to see Romeo Remey standing in his door.

"Someone to see you."

Romeo backed away and Jim Anderson walked into Luc's office.

Well, this is interesting, Luc thought as he stood up.

"May I help you, Monsieur Anderson?" Luc said.

"Yes, you can release Madame Cazaly this minute. I'm here to tell you that Madame C is no more a murderer than poor old Sister Amelie at *l'église*. Are you so desperate to prove yourself that you're willing to let an old woman hang for a crime everyone knows she didn't commit?"

To say Luc was surprised at Anderson's outburst would be an understatement. His first inclination was to ask him if Jules knew he was here. His second inclination was to ask how close he was to the family since Madame Cazaly had been released yesterday. In the end he knew Anderson's mission today had nothing to do with Madame Cazaly and he'd be wasting everyone's time pretending it did.

Anderson was as obvious as a child. *Or perhaps this is what passes for courting in the United States.*

Anderson wants to be a hero in Jules' eyes.

That is not going to happen.

"I've registered your comments," Luc said impassively, returning to his desk in a dismissive gesture. He waited a moment, finally glancing up as soon as it became clear that Anderson wasn't leaving.

"There is more you wish to say, Monsieur?"

"I think you should know that Jules and I are together," Anderson said.

Luc felt his face flush. Just hearing the words triggered the response. He hoped Anderson was too insensitive to detect it. Most American men would be.

"I thought you should know," Anderson said, "in case you thought you still had a chance with her. We're sleeping together. So if you did have any ideas in her direction, well, you can give it up."

Luc felt a smile coming on.

"I think you wouldn't have to say such a thing to me if the lady were truly yours," Luc said.

Anderson scowled. "We do things differently where Jules and I come from," Anderson said. "I'm giving you the benefit of the doubt. I'm just telling you. Don't test her."

"Why? Because she might weaken?"

"No, that's not what I meant. And don't test *me* either."

"You do know who you're talking to?"

"I assume you wouldn't use your position as chief of the Chabanel police to hamstring me," Anderson said, but his face had flushed uncomfortably. "This is strictly man-to-man. Nothing to do with your role as head village cop."

Luc shrugged. "Rest assured. There is nothing between me and Jules."

"Great. I'm just saying let's keep it that way."

Luc shrugged again, this time with a smile that he genuinely felt.

"That is up to Jules," he said. "The kiss last night was unanticipated to be sure. But I will be ready the minute she is."

Anderson sputtered and groped for words that up to now had been in French.

"You...did she...is that a threat?" he finally said in English.

"Let's call it a *heads up*, as you say in your country. And now, Monsieur." Luc pointed to the door and after a long moment Anderson turned on his heel.

"You'd better release Madame Cazaly!" Anderson said over his shoulder. "That's all I came to say!"

Luc shook his head and went back to studying the lab report. But for some reason he felt better than he had in days.

23

SYMPATHY FOR THE DEVIL

I rode home in the dark glad for the battery of my little bike light. That was about all I was glad for. While getting the info from Eloise that Chevalier had been killed with a fast-acting deadly poison was very helpful, finding out that the leaves for making that poison had been found *in our éclair booth* was less than positive news.

I struggled to pedal the last few yards up the gravel drive leading to *La Fleurette*. The heavy rain had created puddles and shifted mud onto the drive. As it was I was going to have to toss my shoes and jacket straight into the wash.

And by *wash* I mean, the big wooden tub where I would be able to find them in the morning to scrub and rinse them out by hand.

Sigh. I'd heard the rumors that parts of Provence were going to get electricity again and I personally could think of few things more desperately necessary than electric washing machines, followed close behind by a working oven that didn't require me to feed sticks into it every few minutes.

I came in through the front door, careful not to slip on

the granite foyer tiles in my wet shoes. I pulled them off and tossed them in the rubber bin by the door and made it nearly to the kitchen before Cocoa leapt onto my knees desperate to greet me.

"Hey, girl," I said, stopping long enough to pet her. "You had your dinner?"

"Jules, *c'est toi*?" Madame B called from the kitchen.

I pulled off my sodden denim jacket and hung it on one of the dowels that the sisters kept in the kitchen for towels. The warm glimmer of light from two large kerosene lanterns drew me into the kitchen.

"Oh! *Tu es trop trempé!*" Madame B said when she saw me. "*As-tu faim?*"

I *was* hungry. In addition to the soup I'd spent most of my few remaining euros on a tiny plate of *gougères* that I let Eloise eat most of in order to keep her talking.

The aroma of a garlicky *ratatouille* wafted enticingly around the room.

"*Assieds toi*," Madame B said indicating the kitchen table. A place setting was laid out for me. The sisters must have already eaten.

There is something very bone-deep satisfying about coming home in the dark—tired, wet, and discouraged—to find a glowing light in the kitchen and a hot home-cooked dinner on the table. It is one of the singular most wonderful experiences of my life and before I got stuck in France with no friends, no lights, no money and just the clothes on my back, I had never experienced it before.

I sat down as Madame B ladled the *ratatouille* into my bowl. Cocoa took up her place at my knee. I looked around.

"Where's Léa?"

"*Endormi.* Do you want wine?"

Sleeping made sense. Confessing to murder must be exhausting when you're in your nineties.

"Sure. Wine sounds great. Join me?"

Madame B brought the wine bottle, two glasses and a baton of fresh bread to the table. She poured our wine and sat with me as I ate my dinner. When I was finished, I folded my napkin and looked at her.

"Please tell me again why Madame C would do this," I said softly.

Madame B sighed. "I told you. It is the guilt."

"But that was so long ago. And what she's doing now will not undo it. All it does is let the true murderer go free."

I held Madame B's gaze. She looked tired. She looked worried.

"Is that what she wants?" I asked.

"She wants to sleep at night."

"What about us? What about you? Is she really going to leave us?"

"She knows we will take care of each other."

"What about if I try to run off to America again?"

"You won't do that now."

It was frankly astonishing to me that she just assumed I'd throw away any and all chances to go back to my own country. Her generation had a deep sense of responsibility. A dangerously deep sense of responsibility. Right out of an Austen novel in fact. And here she was giving me the benefit of the doubt that I felt the same way.

"So you're okay with Madame C going to prison?" I asked.

"I am accepting it."

"What she's doing doesn't help anyone."

"It helps Madame Zabala who is now free."

Talking with her was useless. I knew that. I don't know why I continued to try.

"Madame Zabala's grandson has been arrested," I said.

Madame B made a sharp intake of breath. "*Non!*"

"Someone saw him skulking around our place so he's being held on suspected arson."

"Why would he do this?" She seemed genuinely perplexed. I love Justine Becque. She really does see the good in everyone. On second thought, I'm not sure that's a positive trait.

"Justine, the poison that was used to kill the chef is called foxglove."

She nodded politely.

"And it was found in bulk in our booth."

Honestly, I knew going in that she wasn't going to understand all that. She frowned and I had to go find the French English dictionary I'd stolen from the Chabanel library a few months back to look up the word *poison*. Turns out it's the same in French as it is in English.

"How...how is this possible?" she asked, stunned.

"You tell me."

"I am as surprised as you."

"Well, I'm sure *that's* not true but it confirms something I'd already figured out—the poison was planted in our booth."

Madame B frowned at this and we went through the whole dictionary thing one more time. I did think it was important for her to know that it wasn't just Madame Cazaly who was intent on hanging herself.

Someone else out there was trying to help her do it.

When Madame B finally got the gist of *that* implication she leaned away from me and began to rock.

I suppose it's one thing to choose to sacrifice your life for your specific set of ideals or reasons but it is quite another for someone else to do it for you. I could see the idea of someone deliberately trying to fit the noose around her sister's neck didn't sit well with Madame B. Not at all. Not one bit.

"Who would have done such a thing?" she finally asked.

"Oh, gee, Justine, I don't know. Maybe the real murderer?"

~

Luc walked out of the meeting with Eloise, Matteo and Romeo. It had been a long day and much that had begun unresolved was still, frustratingly, unresolved.

For the first time in weeks, Luc decided to go back to his own apartment for the night—to give himself a chance to step away and see if that didn't help clear his head.

Were they really sleeping together?

He tried to dismiss the thought. Anderson had come to score points with Jules by pleading for Madame C's release. That was all. Nothing more to it.

As Luc packed a valise for the night, he heard Tristan screaming down the hall from his jail cell. The boy had been alternately shouting obscenities and napping all afternoon and Luc had to admit it was as much the desire for a good night's sleep that had him packing it in for the night.

If Tristan was like most young people, he wouldn't settle down for hours yet. Luc needed a moment to talk with Tristan—really talk to him. And that would be better tomorrow after the young man had screamed himself into exhaustion. The last thing Luc wanted to do was hand the kid over to juvenile detention in Lyons which was likely the next step.

Matteo was on duty tonight again and while there was something about the way he interacted with Tristan that didn't feel quite right to Luc, he was too tired to examine it in detail tonight.

Tomorrow. Plenty of time to get to the bottom of it all tomorrow.

That night, just after midnight, Luc was awakened by Romeo Remey's energetic pounding on his apartment door.

Tristan Zabala had been discovered dead in his cell.

24

MISSION CRITICAL

That morning I woke to the sight of both Madame Twins leaning over my bed in the still darkened morning. They'd gotten the terrible news about Tristan from old Monsieur Augustin who delivers milk in his donkey cart.

They made me a cup of coffee which I drank after I dressed and we all hurried out of the house and down the long, dark road toward Chabanel. It was a cold morning—as all mornings in mid October are now—but I barely registered the fact, so stunned was I at the news that Tristan had been found dead in his cell last night.

My mind was a whirl as we walked into town toward the police station. The sisters said nothing except a few murmured words to each other that I didn't understand. They both hesitated as we passed the street where Madame Zabala lived but didn't stop.

As we arrived at the *place de la maire*, I was surprised to see that even in the early morning there were at least half a dozen people gathered in front of the police station.

God knows who spread the word. Perhaps it was the prying eyes of neighbors who saw Sergeant Basile make the middle of the night trip to Madame Zabala's house to inform her as next of kin. That would do it. A midnight visit from the police would be enough to have half the village up and aware by breakfast.

Theo Bardot was handing out coffee to the people gathered, as well as to the police—Romeo Remey and Matteo—both of whom stood outside the station.

As I looked at Matteo I was reminded again of Nicole's claim. Watching him now as he glared at the crowd of people in the square, I couldn't help but think there was more to this—more to him—than I was seeing.

Was Tristan murdered? Did he kill himself?

I searched the crowd for Madame Zabala but of course she would be inside with Luc. And the body.

Was this a coincidence that Chevalier was killed three days ago and now Tristan? And was that coincidence really believable?

I watched the crowd—all hungry for news—some with fearful looks on their faces as if whatever had happened to Chevalier and Tristan might be catching—or worse. Was there a serial killer on the loose? Were the two deaths connected?

The Madame Twins stayed quietly by my side—a first for both of them. I tried to study Madame C's face to see if Tristan's death somehow played into her own guilt about his family and Madame Zabala but as usual, her expression was completely closed.

The rain had stopped and as the clouds started to scuttle away I could see the morning light begin to illuminate the cobblestones, the ancient fountain in the square and the empty stone planters.

Today would be a nice day. One way or another it would definitely be a picnic day for me and Jim.

As I thought of Jim, I turned to look behind me and was surprised to see Enora Roche standing by the fountain in the square, a steaming cup of coffee in one hand.

Maybe I shouldn't have been surprised to see her here.

Beside Enora was Madame Fournier, who was leaning over and talking to her.

Talking to her in a *very* intimate way.

25

A SHORT LEASH

Ever notice how when things come together you can actually hear the pieces clicking?

That's what I heard when I saw Madame Fournier and Enora Roche, their heads together conspiratorially.

They weren't enemies. They were *together*!

Suddenly it all made sense. The two of them must have killed Chevalier. Why wouldn't they? He was an abusive pig who'd harmed them both and they were clearly into each other.

They got rid of Chevalier....I chewed my lip as I thought of this. But why? It didn't really make sense that they'd kill Chevalier in order to be together. Why couldn't they just be together?

And then there was the Tristan factor.

Did they kill Tristan too? Why would they? How did they even *know* him? Maybe Tristan knew something and they were trying to keep him quiet? Had they paid Tristan off? Is that where he got the money I saw him spending at

Theo's café? Had he been paid to keep quiet about something he saw?

As soon as I started down this mental road, all impasses seemed to melt away. I couldn't believe I hadn't thought of it before.

It was so obvious!

Enora Roche and Madame Fournier were the killers!

Madame Fournier had motive, opportunity and means—she could easily have tampered with Madame Zabala's éclairs. And it would explain why Enora didn't taste the éclair when she was first in line to do that.

She knew the éclair had been poisoned because her lover had done the poisoning!

The door to the station opened and Luc came out and raised his hands to speak to the crowd. The moment I saw him my heart began to race. He looked like he hadn't had any sleep. His brown hair was ruffled and uncombed and he hadn't shaved yet.

Worst of all, I saw his lips—grim and frowning—and the memory of them on mine just two nights before made me tingle like a schoolgirl.

He spoke in rapid, smooth French to everyone gathered and I cursed the fact that my language skills weren't good enough to understand what he was saying. I grabbed Madame B's arm.

"What's he saying? Is he saying how Tristan died? Was it suicide?"

But Madame B waved me away in order to concentrate on what Luc was saying. In frustration, I looked around the crowd and saw Jim making his way toward me. I hurried over to him and he took me in his arms and gave me a long hug.

I broke away. I guess he thought he needed to console

me for some reason but I needed him interpreting for me at the moment.

"What is Luc saying?" I asked breathlessly as I pulled away. "Was it suicide?"

Jim frowned and a spasm of hurt flashed across his face but he recovered quickly.

"He's asking everyone to go home and respect Madame Zabala's privacy," Jim said.

I should have known Luc wouldn't give away any actual information but it was still annoying. The group started to break up and I turned to see Enora and Marie Fournier but they had already slipped away.

"So are you up for the picnic tonight?" Jim asked. "I think the weather's finally cleared."

Before I could answer, I caught the eye of Madame C, who arched an eyebrow at me in a very disproving way. I don't know why I worry about bothering to learn this language. Both the Madame Twins have no trouble communicating with me at all. It appeared that on top of their disapproval over my dating Jim was their belief that I was using him to my own ends.

Were they right? Was I using Jim? Why would I? Who was I benefiting by using him?

I was thinking this at the very moment—I kid you not—when the memory of Luc's kiss came to me and just as I noticed that the crowd had thinned enough where Luc had a direct line of sight on me.

Our eyes met like some sort of cheesy rom-com moment, the sudden passion of which jolted me like an electric shock. Flustered, I forced myself to look away from him. When I did, Jim slipped his arm around my shoulders and kissed me.

Which, of course, is a totally appropriate thing for us to do, after all, being a couple and all.

When I stole another quick glance at Luc, I saw he was busy talking to one of the village women.

I felt a rush of relief that he hadn't seen the kiss. But also I felt relief because my guilty reaction to it meant I *wasn't* trying to make Luc jealous.

Somehow, for Jim's sake, that was important to me.

26

BACK BURNER

Luc was sick with self-loathing.

If only he'd talked to Tristan last night before leaving the station. Would he have caught the signs in time? Would he have been able to see that the boy was ill?

He tightened his hand on Eloise's shoulder. His sergeant stood beside him in his office, tears streaking down her face. She'd been the one to bring Tristan his dinner last night, a dinner which had largely gone uneaten and was now bagged and on its way to the forensics lab in Ecully.

Had she unwittingly delivered poison to him?

And did that mean that Tristan was murdered? Or had they not checked him well enough when they arrested him for poison on his person? Had he killed himself?

Why would he do that?

Tristan had been very angry when Luc saw him last. He was always angry.

But despondent?

"We'll find the answers," he said to Eloise in an attempt to console her. "It wasn't your fault."

Eloise sniffled and nodded but Luc was sure he hadn't helped. She felt responsible. She had walked the food into his cell, put it down before him and now Tristan was dead.

The thought of it served to further ignite the fury bubbling in Luc's chest. How could there be so few clues? The frustration of not being able to rely on science to tell them what happened was intense and unrelenting.

And seeing Jules kiss Anderson like that, well, that hadn't helped either.

~

An hour later, after saying *adieu* to Jim and nailing down definite plans for meeting later this evening for our big picnic, I walked back to *La Fleurette* with the twins. The sisters were more talkative on the way home but I was just as clueless about what they were saying. Since there was no way they could know more than I did at this point, I didn't sweat it.

Back home, Madame C went immediately to the garden to pull weeds and do whatever she needed to work out her frustrations. Madame B went to the kitchen. That was my cue to get the ovens hot again. It had been a couple of days since the fête and all the nonstop baking we'd been doing so the twins had given the ovens a rest. We'd been eating cold food but it was autumn and that couldn't last for long.

Madame B began chopping up the vegetables she'd taken from the garden to make a stew. I wasn't sure if it was a meat stew since fresh meat only came when you least expected it. Gone were the days when you could just run to the butcher and count on him having anything.

As I moved out onto the patio, Cocoa at my heels, I sent another silent prayer skyward that electricity was coming back soon. I had a fairly decent stack of firewood and kindling on the side of the house—covered against the rain—which I went to first. Normally, if we'd had a dry couple of days I'd be out foraging for wood but I knew it would all be wet now so I didn't bother.

Sometimes I amaze myself at how my life has changed. If I had thought six months ago that I'd think nothing at all of rummaging around the countryside for wood to fuel an oven so I could eat a stew with no meat in it and be thrilled—well, it was unthinkable.

My life has changed so much, so completely. How is it possible to say in spite of all that's happened that I'm happy?

And yet, weirdly, I am.

After stuffing the outdoor oven with dry wood and getting it lit—always an accomplishment—I sat on the patio and stared at the pieces of wood inside the kiln crackling and popping.

Cocoa was in the woods doing her rounds of checking on rabbits and skunks and the like. The bunnies and other woodland creatures were so cute around here that, meatless weeks or not, I was not at the point where I was okay trapping and eating them.

I must have been wrapped in my thoughts a good thirty minutes when the French doors opened from the kitchen and none other than Agathe Zabala walked outside. I was astonished to see her but in retrospect I shouldn't have been.

She'd had a terrible shock this morning. Well, maybe not all that terrible. I'm not trying to be ugly but Tristan had been heading down a particular path for a while now and to end up dead couldn't have been a very big shock to most people.

I know. I'm going to burn in hell for my ungenerous nature. The Madame Twins tell me as much all the time.

I jumped up when I saw Madame Zabala and she waved me tiredly to sit back down. She sat next to me and pulled out a packet of cigarettes and lit one up. It always surprises me when anybody in Chabanel smokes—Luc for one—since it's so unusual in the States these days. But it especially surprises me when someone Madame Zabala's age does it. A part of me wanted to say *how is it you've lived this long as a smoker? Is the whole lung cancer thing a big PR lie by the government? Or are you just a walking miracle?*

You know the French paradox? Oh, I'm here to tell you it exists, baby. In spades.

So I watched Madame Zabala puff away, pretty much ignoring me and having her own thoughts—no doubt about Tristan—and I tried to frame how I would ask her my questions because make no mistake, I had questions.

Madame B came outside to see how well—or not—the fire was going. She thumped a heavy black-bottomed pot on top of the grill and used an iron poker to stir the fire. Luc used to tell me that breaking up the sticks in the fire just served to dissipate the heat so maybe she wanted to bring the temperature down.

Have I mentioned how badly I want electricity to come back to my world? Can you imagine just twisting a little dial and *voila*! you get a few degrees difference in heat? If we get electricity again I promise to never be anything but grateful for that one thing alone.

"I'm sorry about what happened to Tristan," I said to Madame Zabala.

"Jules, *laisse-la tranquille*," Madame B said sternly. *Leave her alone.* She raised that famous Gallic eyebrow at me and then left.

I could see Madame C was still pulling weeds in the far corner of the garden. She probably didn't even know Madame Zabala was here.

"*Merci*," Madame Zabala said, not looking at me as she smoked.

"*Comme il mort?*" I asked. I know that wasn't correct French but I also knew she'd get the gist of it. *How did he die?*

"*Poison.*"

I have to say it's so helpful when the French word for a thing is the same as the English word.

But wow. Tristan was poisoned? Like Chevalier?

I felt a fluttering lightness in my chest and I leaned toward Madame Zabala.

"You speak English?" I asked.

She made that hand rocking gesture the French love so much because it means yes and no and also so-so.

I was so excited to imagine that she might be able to speak to me in my own language that it took me a moment to get my thoughts together.

"How did you learn English?"

"I am working in Paris after the war," she said and stubbed out her cigarette against the pavers. "American GIs." She gave me an implacable look.

"Was Tristan's death…an accident?"

She snorted and looked out over the *potager*. I followed her glance. Madame C had stood up and was looking back at us. She'd seen Madame Zabala. My private chat might be coming to a close.

"Do the police think someone killed Tristan?" I asked hurriedly, hating the fact that I was speaking quickly now. As soon as Madame C came over here, my window of opportunity would be over.

"I do not know," Madame Zabala said tiredly.

I decided to take a different tact. She may not know what Luc was thinking but surely she knew what *she* was thinking. I needed to find out if Tristan's mystery man—especially if it was Matteo—was germane to what happened to Tristan.

"Was Tristan gay?"

"I don't know this word."

"Did he prefer men sexually?"

"How in the world would I know such a thing?"

"Well, did he have a good relationship with his father?"

"I'm sure he never knew his father." She pulled another cigarette out of her packet and lit it. I glanced back at the garden and saw that for whatever reason—miraculously—Madame C had decided not to join us.

Before I could push the point with Madame Zabala, Madame B came back out of the house and set down a platter of raw vegetables for grilling beside the stove. She gave me a suspicious look but since Madame Zabala didn't appear upset, Madame B said nothing and returned to the kitchen.

"*Les soeurs* have welcomed me to stay with them," Madame Zabala said almost bitterly. "Chief DeBray insisted I not be alone. Idiotic."

"Why are you and *les soeurs* at odds?" I asked softly. "They won't tell me or maybe my French isn't good enough to understand them."

Of course I *did* know. I just wanted to hear it from Madame Zabala.

"It is a secret," Madame Zabala said. "A terrible secret that haunts Léa Cazaly."

I didn't say anything—a tactic I'd read about to keep people talking which, I must say, is a particularly difficult practice for me to master. But it works. Every time.

"Léa has never known true love," Madame Zabala said, puffing angrily on her cigarette, the creases around her mouth deepening as she took each harsh drag. "It is for this reason she needed to punish me."

Interesting perspective. I'm not sure she's wrong.

"You had a great love?" I prompted.

Instantly her eyes softened as she stared toward the horizon of the fields. Her voice dropped.

"A great love," she said.

"Tell me."

And so she did. And as she spoke, I heard more and more clicks and thunks in my head as the pieces to the puzzle snapped seamlessly into place.

Tristan was Madame Zabala's great grandchild—just as Jim and I had deduced. She had become pregnant at the end of the war—which I already knew. She'd given birth to a girl, Gigi, who ran off, became pregnant at thirteen and gave birth herself to a daughter before committing suicide.

That baby—a daughter—had grown up only to die early of cancer but not before she had herself, a child. Tristan.

Homeless, orphaned and born with a disfiguring hair lip, the boy lived on the streets in Lyons making his way any way he could until he found his way back to Chabanel and his maternal great grandmother.

That was two years ago when he was fourteen. During that time he lived in *Mégisseries* and worked to disrupt Madame Zabala's life in every way that he could.

"He was no joy to me," she said stonily. "He was created to punish me. As were his mother and his grandmother."

"Punish you for what?" I asked softly, hoping not to destroy the delicate trance that kept her remembering...and talking.

"My crime."

Ah. The German officer. Tristan's great grandfather.

The way *les soeurs* told the story, Madame Zabala gave herself to the Germans in order to get information out of them. A sudden thought came to me. *What if you found yourself falling in love with the enemy? You might think you deserved every terrible thing that happened to you after that.*

"Did you love him?"

"What is love? I thought I did. I certainly gave up everything for him."

I gave her a moment and guilt rushed through me. Was all this necessary to know? Was this going to find Chevalier's killer? Or Tristan's? Or dissuade Madame C from insisting she was a murderer?

"What happened to him?" I asked.

"He went back to Germany."

"And you never heard from him again?"

"He had a family there."

"Oh."

"Not very romantic, eh?"

"And then your own people turned on you."

She looked at me and her eyes cleared. Now she knew that I knew she'd been punished by the village. And she knew I knew it had been on the say so of Madame Cazaly.

"It was a different time," she said finally. "A foolish girl in love was not considered much of an excuse for fraternizing with *la Bosch*."

"I'm sorry, Madame Zabala," I said. "The village was wrong. And you weren't foolish. You were brave."

She looked at me and her eyes filled with tears. "*Merci*," she said quietly.

I got up and stirred the pot of vegetables. I could see Madame B watching from the window in the kitchen. She wouldn't come out if she thought I was minding the stew.

Madame C was standing up again, massaging her back and watching us.

"Did Chief DeBray tell you what kind of poison killed Tristan?" I asked. I watched Madame C toss down her hoe and turn toward us.

Madame Zabala wiped her eyes and took in a long breath.

"He said the lab must take its time."

"So he didn't know if the poison was put in Tristan's food at the police station? Or done earlier?"

I could hear the sound of Madame C's footsteps as she came nearer and nearer.

"He believed it had been...given to Tristan before his arrest."

That made sense. Slow-acting poison. It would have been too easy to trace if the food at the station had been tampered with. I felt a rush of relief for poor Eloise who I knew must have been horrified to think that Tristan died on her watch. Right under her nose. Maybe even with the food she'd served him.

At least this way—if it was true that it was slow-acting—there was probably nothing anyone could have done.

As Madame C joined us and immediately opened the stew pot and began stirring it—without a word to Madame Zabala—I sat back on the hard stone bench, my mind spinning with all that Madame Zabala had told me.

So much guilt and blame and shame! And so long ago!

Could it really have anything to do with what was happening right now? And if so, did that mean the killer was done?

Or just getting started?

27

SOMETHING IN THE WAY SHE MOVES

Lunch at *La Fleurette* was quite the somber affair that afternoon. Madame Zabala may have been invited to stay at *La Fleurette* but the issue between her and Madame C was as viable and alive as ever. I have no idea what was going through either of their heads while they were passing the grilled eggplant and the *aïoli*.

I couldn't take the bizarre, tension-laden silence for long and escaped after the last dish was served, even eschewing the *tarte tropézienne* that was coming so you *know* how bad it must have been.

I rode my bike back into Chabanel with the express purpose of either waylaying Luc for more info on what happened—not really a happy prospect—or seeing if I could find Marie Fournier and Enora Roche for a more up-close analysis of whatever the hell they were up to.

Let's face it, Tristan had been my lead suspect on the Chevalier murder right up to the moment when he ended up dead by the same method and Macbeth's three witches—or in this case two—showed up to gloat.

In fact, the more I thought about it, Tristan had

never been a good suspect. He didn't know enough about poisons—or éclairs—to kill Chevalier. Plus, it was hardly the kind of murder weapon most sixteen-year-old boys would opt for and, like Jim said, it was way too planned and deliberate for someone as wild as Tristan.

Taking Tristan out of the equation and ignoring both Madame Cazaly and Madame Zabala's unlikely involvement, you were left with Enora Roche and Marie Fournier.

Why didn't I see it before?

As I rode to town I did my best to recall the day of the fête and I saw again in my mind how the two judges had edged their way around the perimeter of the booths, taking turns judging the cakes, tarts and *profiteroles* at each booth. I tried to remember who had gotten a ribbon just before they went to Madame Zabala's booth and I was sure—I could literally see it in my mind!—that it was Lucien who'd handed it out.

That meant that Enora *should* have been first to taste Madame Zabala's éclairs.

But if that was so, why didn't *Enora* eat the éclair and die?

Either she was the killer—definitely a possibility—or she was the intended victim. But if that was true why didn't the murderer try again?

Suddenly I realized there was a third possibility.

Either Enora was the killer or she was the intended victim, *or* she smelled that something was wrong with the éclair and *let Lucien go ahead and eat it knowing he wouldn't be able to detect the poison because of his cold.*

I found myself getting excited. One way or the other Enora knew the éclair was poisoned and let Lucien Chevalier eat it and die.

I shivered when I thought how close Jim and I had come to eating the deadly éclair.

Did that mean the murder was random? Did it matter to the murderer *who* was killed? Are we looking for someone who hated Lucien when that wasn't a part of the equation?

With no motive against a specific victim, it meant the murderer could be anyone. And that would be an interesting theory except for one thing.

Killing Tristan was not random.

I rode by Madame Fournier's bakery and saw that it was closed. She hadn't yet set up a third plate of glass to replace the second one that I'd broken and the shop looked forlorn and deserted. I glanced at the apartment over the shop and saw that a light was on. Normally that wouldn't necessarily mean that she was home. Nowadays, however, only a fool left a kerosene lantern on when they weren't home.

Unless Enora Roche was up there too, this meant I had a chance to talk to her alone at her hotel.

Chabanel only had one hotel and I think it's a stretch to even call it that. It had once been a private residence and while never opulent by anyone's standards, it was large and had not fallen down into decay as had so many other large buildings in Chabanel that the state hadn't commandeered for various purposes.

I parked my bike next to the *charcuterie* which was now only open about once a week, and then usually only to sell rabbits, sheep and chicken. If people wanted beef—which they rarely did in Provence even before the EMP—they went to the black market for it. Thinking of the black market made me think of Nicole and Tristan.

I wondered if there would be anyone on that side of the tracks who would mourn Tristan. I made a mental note to ask Eloise for a photo of Matteo. Someday soon I'd go back to *Mégisseries* and show it to Nicole to find out the answer to the enigmatic older mystery man once and for all.

I went into the hotel where Monsieur Bonnet was standing at the registration desk flipping through a magazine that had to be at least five months old. He looked up at me and frowned.

"*Le chambre de Madame Roche*?" I said with a smile.

He grimaced at me as if he'd eaten a bad oyster so I guess it should have been *la chambre* but it could just as easily have been my smile. Or the fact that I was American. Or maybe female? I had long ago given up wondering why some French people take an instant dislike to me. Half the time it has nothing to do with me. Well, maybe a fourth of the time.

"*Vingt-deux*," he said and went back to his magazine.

I headed for the stairs. I'm not sure why they put Enora on the second floor when I know for a fact that there's zero other people living in the hotel. Madame B and C were constantly saying they expect the hotel to close any day now and they have no idea what old Monsieur Bonnet will do then.

Probably stay in the customer service industry since he's so good with people.

As I walked down the hall toward Enora Roche's room I wondered if Enora had always been gay or if her time with Chevalier had simply turned her against all men. It had been a surprise to see her with Marie Fournier and not just because I hadn't picked up on her being gay but also because Jim had mentioned that he thought she'd come on to him.

Of course, in my experience most men have no clue about *who* is coming on to *whom*. It was sweet that Jim thought that, I thought. But he probably just caught Enora blinking a cinder out of her eye and thought it was a wink in his direction.

The thought made me smile but it also made my stomach clench in anticipation of the "talk" I now knew Jim and I were headed for. He was such a sweet man and he deserved better than being caught in the middle of whatever was going on with me. It wasn't fair to him.

I stood in front of Enora's hotel room door and listened. I didn't hear voices but I did hear someone moving around inside. I knocked firmly and was rewarded by Enora jerking open the door, her face flushed with euphoric anticipation —until she saw it was me.

"Well, well," I said in my finest villain's smirk. "Expecting someone else?"

She tried to shut the door but I stuck my foot in it.

"I need to talk with you," I said.

"*Je ne parle pas l'anglais,*" she said.

It really bugs me how many times people try to pull the ol' *can't speak English* card on me. Damned annoying.

"No problem-o," I said. "*Moi, je parle francais.*" Of course I couldn't speak French worth a crap. Certainly not at the level where I would be able to ask the questions I needed to ask. I felt an irrational splinter of anger at Luc.

Why wasn't he working with me? Why did he always treat me as a hindrance? It occurred to me that I could have brought Jim to interpret for me but honestly he was usually not totally on board either for my sleuthing activities.

Why is it the people I need to understand this stupid language for me are never with me when I need them? I resolved to fast-track my French learning in the next few months to never feel this kind of frustration again.

"Look," I said, "er, *regardez* Madame Roche but I...I mean, *vous* need to know that *je suis totalement* aware of who you are with and why you...*vous* killed...er *la morte* Lucien Chevalier." Damn. What was the word for murder? You'd think that would be the first word I'd learn since coming to Chabanel.

Enora Roche looked at me as if I'd lost my mind. She did not look frightened or intimidated in any way.

"You go," she said evenly, "or me call police."

And then she slammed the door in my face.

I stood there for a moment thinking her English was almost as bad as my French. But mostly I stood there, immobilized with shock, my mind whirling, because just before she shut the door I'd caught a glimpse of something on the dresser behind her.

Something that didn't belong there.

Something that the killer of both Chevalier and Tristan would have needed.

I saw a syringe.

28

THE WEAKEST LINK

A syringe was how the poison had been injected into the éclair! How else? It was the perfect murder weapon. Without ready access to DNA analysis, it could be washed out or just tossed away. Plus it could easily have been hidden in Enora's clothes as she approached Madame Zabala's pastry booth.

Then with a quick distraction of Madame Zabala, Enora could have swiftly injected the poison into the éclair with no one the wiser.

As I hurried back down the stairs and out of the hotel, I couldn't wait to present what I'd discovered to Luc. I knew he'd balk—after all, as per usual, *I'd* found the key evidence that would lead to the real murderer—but I also knew Luc was fair and he'd come around.

I felt a flush of pleasure as I considered these handful of Luc's many positive traits.

And that was *not* what I wanted to be thinking of at the moment.

I glanced at my watch as I grabbed my bike and realized

I didn't have time to go find Luc, lay out my evidence and also run home to change before my date with Jim tonight.

Grimy, rumpled clothes and most of my makeup sweated off down my chin?

Oh, well. Perhaps it was for the best if I didn't look too desirable for the conversation I was going to have with Jim.

But still. Not to dress up for a date?

It took everything I had to pedal toward the *police municipale* and not back to *La Fleurette*.

∽

Marie Fournier knocked on the hotel door momentarily reliving the last time she'd been here when she'd snuck up the fire escape and crept down the hall so that no one would see.

She remembered the look on Enora's face when she'd opened the door to her and erased all doubt from Marie's mind about the look the two of them had shared that day—the day Lucien was killed.

It was the look of love that Marie had been hungering for six long years and, after a night of tears and promises in the hotel, it became clear that it had been much the same for Enora.

And finally they were together.

The door opened hesitantly and Enora cried out when she saw Marie and flung herself into the other woman's arms.

Enora was shaking.

Instantly Marie led Enora back into the room and settled her on the bed.

"That horrible American woman is telling the police

that I am involved in Lucien's murder!" Enora said through her tears.

"No! I don't believe it! Why? What does she know?"

"Nothing! She knows nothing! But she can cause problems."

Marie sat on the bed and gnawed a nail, trying to think. What did this mean? Should they take action? Should they do nothing?

"The American man was in the shop yesterday," Marie said. "He was shopping for a special picnic he and the other American are having."

"Americans are so crass," Enora said with disgust. "Telling the world their private business. They have no sense of propriety."

"Yes, but I think in this case we may benefit from that."

"How?"

"He bragged to everyone in the *boulangerie* exactly where this picnic would be."

Enora went very still. "You know where the two of them will be? Alone?"

Marie nodded grimly. "It is a remote area. There is a waterfall nearby."

Enora nodded. "So screams would be drowned out."

"They would."

Enora took her hand. "Can we do this?"

"I think we must, *chérie*. We just need to be strong for a little bit longer."

"I will do it, Marie. You don't need to be there."

"No, we will do it together, *chérie*."

29

THERE OUGHTA BE A LAW

The good news? Matteo wasn't in the office. The bad news? Luc was in the office and he wasn't happy.

Once I arrived at the station, the portly and grumpy station receptionist Madame Gabin called for Luc to come see me in the waiting room. In the old days I would have been ushered back to his office for a private conference. Now I was standing in the middle of six villagers with complaints ranging from farm vandal to petty theft.

I waited a quarter of an hour before Luc came out and motioned for me to come to the front door.

The better to toss me out, I guess.

"What is it?" he said tiredly.

"I wanted to know if you'd talked to Enora Roche about Chevalier's murder," I said crisply. I assumed not too many of the people in the waiting room spoke English but it still bugged me not to get a private audience.

"She is not a person of interest."

"Have you even talked to her? I did just now and caught

her with a syringe. A *syringe*, Luc, which in case you need me to remind you is probably the murder weapon."

Luc sighed noisily and indicated by a jerk of his head that I was, after all, to follow him some place less public. He led me to the hallway behind the front sergeant's desk. There was no place to sit so he clearly didn't want either of us to get comfortable.

"Was it clogged full of foxglove leaves when you found it?" he said.

I knew he was being sarcastic which I have to say was extremely annoying but I did a masterful job of ignoring it.

"Not that I could see but I didn't get that close."

"And you think the murderer would just keep the murder weapon laying around on a dresser top?"

He had a point and I began to feel a little warm. For October, they sure kept the heat on high in the police station. Probably for all the confessions they were invariably trying to sweat out of people.

"Well, probably not," I said, "but you have to ask yourself why did she have a syringe at all?"

"Perhaps because she's diabetic."

"A pastry chef who's diabetic," I scoffed. "Is that believable?"

"It is the truth."

My mouth fell open. "So you knew about the syringe?"

"You're wasting my time, Jules. Go home."

"You need to talk to Enora Roche," I persisted. "Why didn't *she* eat the poisoned éclair? How is it that Chevalier went first? Up to then they'd been taking turns—I saw them!—and it wasn't his turn, it was hers. You need to talk to her. And also to Marie Fournier. The two of them are in cahoots."

"I am not knowing this word *cahoots* but in any case I've heard enough."

He swept out a hand to indicate I should follow it in the direction of the door but I wouldn't be put off quite so easily.

"Did you know Tristan was hanging out with an older man from...the village?" I asked.

I wanted so badly to say it was Matteo but to suggest something so outlandish with no proof really *would* get me thrown out.

Luc narrowed his eyes. "What do you know?"

"Tristan was friendly with some guy from Chabanel. Plus all of a sudden he had money right after Chevalier's murder."

Luc frowned. "What are you saying?"

"*Blackmail*, Luc. Tristan saw Roche and Fournier setting up the murder for Chevalier—or gloating about it afterward. That's why he was killed."

"By Enora Roche."

"And Madame Fournier. They're in this together. Why do you think Fournier pointed the finger at Madame C? Why do you think she planted the foxglove in our booth? It was to protect herself because she's the killer."

"And the motive for killing Chevalier?"

"You ought to know the answer to that, Luc. You're French. She did it for love."

"That's absurd. Marie Fournier hated Chevalier."

"Dear God! Not Chevalier!" I said with exasperation. "She's in love with Enora Roche!"

I watched him as he valiantly tried to connect the dots and in the end I knew he wouldn't make it. The lesbian love connection wasn't enough to get me thrown out like accusing his second in command would have been, but as far as Luc was concerned it was nearly as far-fetched.

"Thank you for your information," he said.

"That's it?"

"I'll look into it."

What else could I do? I'd presented my case and he'd listened. But as his face said as clearly as any spoken words possibly could have: *we are done here.*

~

Agathe Zabala put her hand on the dog's head, making sure the creature would not bark. The dog had been particularly welcoming to her in the two days she'd spent at *La Fleurette.*

Justine had tried and perhaps in her own way so had Léa, but the severity of Agathe's crime had always been there between them. Even Tristan's death—the final piece of physical evidence of her shame—hadn't lessened the weight of her guilt.

No, killing had never helped, no matter how clearly it seemed that it might.

But Agathe knew there was another action that would.

Silently she let herself out the back of the house, making sure the dog couldn't follow her, and stepped into the garden. Behind the low stone walls she saw the fog and mist of the evening hovering over the fields beyond.

She'd always known the secret to erasing every vestige of her crime. And as stupidly as Léa had gone about attempting to find her own peace, in the end Agathe knew there was only one true way to it.

She crossed the uneven slate patio to the far gate, moving slowly. She mustn't trip or fall.

Now more than ever, when she was so sure, she needed to make sure she reached the other side.

30

THE ONLY THING TO FEAR

Luc watched as Adrien Matteo signed on for his shift that evening. The detective was late, nearly forty minutes. He had a long scratch down his cheek that he joked to Madame Gabin that he'd gotten from his normally docile cat.

Luc thought it odd that a cat would leave only one long scratch.

Eloise had taken up the slack of Matteo's tardiness tonight without complaint—as did most of the people Matteo worked with. He was born in Chabanel and much was tolerated from him for that fact alone. But Luc filed the incident away. Not today, maybe not tomorrow. But soon. When he didn't need the man so much.

There would be a reckoning.

He spoke briefly to Romeo Remey, who would make the evening rounds of securing the village with Matteo repeating it again after midnight.

"Headed home, Chief?" Eloise asked as she shrugged into her raincoat for her walk home.

"Not just yet," Luc said. "One more task to do over at the hotel. Did the official lab report come in on Tristan?"

"I put it on your desk," she said.

"Any surprises?"

"It was arsenic. Slow-acting. He could have been given it in small doses over weeks until it killed him. How long it had been in his system won't be known for months. The lab results for autopsies are backed up."

Luc expected as much. In this new world, he would have to rely as much on luck, guesswork and intuition as facts. But he was relieved for Eloise. The poison had already been inside Tristan, slowly killing him, before he'd ever gotten to the police station.

He said goodnight to Eloise and headed for the hotel. He hated thinking that Lola Beaufait's influence had had so much to do with why he hadn't questioned Roche. He'd talked himself into believing that wasn't the case but as soon as Jules mentioned her he'd felt a shock of dismay—at what he knew he had to do and how he knew Beaufait would react.

And that in itself told him more than he cared to believe.

If Beaufait thought Luc was in her pocket, he must prove to her and to himself that that wasn't the case. While he didn't think what Jules had to say about Roche made a whole lot of sense neither was it complete nonsense. A visit was warranted. A more in-depth questioning. At least that.

Jules. He had to smile at her earnest presentation at the station earlier. How could he not have seen it before? There was no way she was sleeping with Anderson. He could sense it. But then a thought came to him and he hesitated.

Or was this an American thing immune to Luc's sensibilities? Jules acted like she belonged to no one. Did that mean she was sleeping with Anderson and just didn't unconsciously telegraph the fact as a French woman might?

Annoyed now, he shook off these thoughts and strode into the Chabanel hotel, ignoring Bonnet at the front desk. He'd already wasted enough time on the old fool when Bonnet had sent for the police yesterday because he thought he heard noises in the hotel attic.

When Luc reached the second floor he knocked firmly on Roche's room door. Within moments, she swung it open and then gasped in surprise.

As well she might.

Behind her stood Marie Fournier, a glass of wine in one hand, her blouse unbuttoned to her waist. Enora attempted to push the door shut but Luc stopped it with an outstretched arm and stepped into the room.

"This is illegal!" Marie Fournier yelped, as she set her glass down and turned her back to button her blouse.

"What exactly are you doing that is illegal?" Luc asked drily.

Enora ran to Marie Fournier, her expression tremulous and fearful.

"Nothing," Marie said turning and putting a calming hand on Enora's shoulder. "Nothing at all."

Luc turned to Enora—clearly the weak link—and spoke sternly.

"The poison that killed your colleague was strong smelling. *You* picked up the éclair first and handed it to him. That was witnessed. That éclair was the murder weapon. Therefore..."

"No!" Enora gasped. "I didn't know!"

"That is not believable," Luc said. "The smell was overwhelming once brought close to your nose which you were seen to do." That last part was a guess but by the look on Enora's face, right on the mark.

"I didn't know it would kill him," she whimpered, looking at Marie as if for strength.

"Leave her alone!" Marie snarled. "You have no proof of anything."

"I have proof in the form of witnesses who will say that Enora Roche picked up the éclair, smelled the poison and then handed it to Lucien Chevalier," Luc said, his pulse racing.

So Jules was right! Enora wasn't innocent. She knew the éclair was off. But whether she was the one who injected the poison...

"She didn't kill him," Marie said forcefully.

Enora slapped her hands to her face and sagged to a sitting position on the bed and began rocking back and forth.

"I knew! I knew!" she sobbed.

Marie knelt by her and took her by the shoulders.

"*Knowing* isn't the same as doing!" Marie said. "For all you knew the chocolate was rancid." She turned and glared at Luc. "She didn't know it was poison."

"But I let him die! Doesn't that make me complicit?" Enora looked between Luc and Marie, her eyes soulful and pleading.

"You couldn't know for sure what you were smelling," Marie said.

"I knew it didn't smell like a chocolate éclair," Enora said sadly.

They both looked at Luc. Perhaps Enora Roche had been merely opportunistic. She knew the éclair was off and she was willing for Chevalier to get sick eating it. But whether she knew it would be fatal was a different matter.

"Don't leave town," he said, turning on his heel and leaving the room.

∽

I'm pretty sure Jim could tell the difference between how I usually dress and how I showed up for our important picnic. He'd left word with Madame B that I was to meet him at the pasture past the old farmer's road behind *La Fleurette* that led to *le petite gorges*, a good two miles away. Madame B wasn't happy delivering the news but seemed cheered by my uncombed hair and the smudges of mud on my damp and wrinkled clothes.

I debated changing clothes but it would have made me way too late and I already felt bad for the boom I was going to lower on ol' Jim. I could hardly make myself look luscious and enticing while I was telling him I just wanted to be friends, now could I?

So when I showed up at the pasture he'd given me directions to—even more bedraggled than when I'd left *La Fleurette*—it was just possible Jim already knew what I was going to say before I even had to say it.

"You look like you've had a hard day," he said manfully, swallowing his disappointment. "A glass of wine is in order."

I looked around at the scene he'd set. He'd gone to major effort for this picnic and my heart sank when I saw it.

A vibrant color-blocked table cloth lay on the ground covered with baskets and china bowls. Where Jim found the perfect little apricots *in November*, I do not know. Or the gorgeous, glossy *fougasse* that is so popular that Madame Fournier sells out of them first thing. There was a quiche, two bottles of wine, a plate of *mille-feuille*—probably one of my most favorite pastries ever—and a basket overflowing with geraniums and begonias.

Why hadn't I just pulled him aside at any of the million and one alleys or doorsteps in Chabanel and told him then? Why did I wait until he'd spent money and effort creating this ridiculously elegant picnic?

Why? Because unlike Jim who was so focused on this big event in our relationship, my mind had been somewhere else all week. And now poor Jim was going to pay the price for that.

Again.

"Wow. This looks amazing," I said, kneeling on the tablecloth and surveying all the foodstuffs, half of which he must have gotten at the black market. That thought sparked an uncomfortable shiver in the back of my mind that I quickly dismissed.

"Yeah, wine would be great," I said.

"Bad day?"

Without thinking—*when will I ever learn to stop doing that?*—I said, "I just had a frustrating conversation with…"

Ever notice how when you suddenly stop your big mouth from yammering on it's almost always too late?

I took a large gulp of wine from my glass.

"Luc?" Jim said. "Is this about the chef's murder? I thought that was all sorted." His voice sounded light but I know him. He wasn't happy. And he wasn't happy *at all* about my nearly saying Luc's name.

"Well, it's just that I had this idea," I said slowly, trying to think of something else to say to switch topics. "And I needed to pass it along to Luc so he—"

"Do you think we could have one evening where Luc DeBray isn't the center of our conversation?"

"He's not the center," I said. "The point I was trying to

make was my new theory about who killed Chevalier and maybe Tristan."

"No, that's just the excuse for you to talk about DeBray or find an excuse to talk *to* DeBray."

"That isn't true." But it sounded true even to my ears. I felt a flush of defensiveness descend over me. I hate being backed into a corner. I suppose everyone does. But as soon as I saw Jim's self-righteous approach to the conversation even I could see I had no defense.

Which just made me want to go on the offense.

So maybe now was a good time to ask him about Nicole? I imagine that would effectively put the kabosh on this whole romantic picnic in a New York second. I could probably even avoid the whole *let's-just-be-friends* thing after that.

Plus it would put *Jim* on the back foot. Just thinking that made me feel like a major coward—trying to unnerve him *before* I broke his heart. Not that he was in love with me. Let's don't dramatize this, I scolded myself. But *however* he felt about me I knew that putting him on the defensive wasn't fair. It was the easy way out and Jim deserved better than that.

"I'm sorry," we both said at the same time. And that just made me feel worse because Jim didn't have anything to apologize for.

"I know I've been preoccupied with creating the perfect moment for us," he said, opening his hands to indicate the beautiful Provencal tablecloth, the dishes of cheese and olives. "I haven't been as present for you and I know you like to bounce your ideas off me."

I squelched my reaction to what sounded like a seriously patronizing comment since my apology was barely out of my mouth. I forced myself to smile instead.

"That's okay," I said, picking up one of the Niçoise olives.

They were so tiny and perfect, so meaty and delicious. They were my favorites.

And the shops in Aix and Chabanel had been out of them for months.

Again the fissure of warning trembled across my mindfield. And again, I waved it away.

"So catch me up," he said. "I'm all ears and all yours tonight." He arched his eyebrows in a funny Groucho Marx impersonation and I laughed as I knew he expected me to.

"Well," I said, "I spoke to Enora Roche today, you know she's the other judge down from Paris?"

Jim nodded as he picked up a salami roll and began to slice it in thin wafers. "What's she still doing in town?" he asked. "Is she a suspect?"

"No, and that's just the point. When I saw her, I also saw a syringe in her room."

"You mean, like what could have been used to inject poison into the éclair?"

"Exactly, yes. Luc...er, I was told that she's diabetic and that's the reason for the syringe but it still seems fishy to me."

"And why is she still in town?"

"You won't believe this. She and Marie Fournier are an item."

"Really? You're kidding."

Something about the way he said that felt false to me. Like he already knew it. But how could he? Last time I talked to him he thought Enora was hot for *him*.

"Anything else?" he asked as he laid out the salami slices on a pretty mustard yellow pottery dish.

"Just that Enora Roche and Marie Fournier make sense for both Chevalier's murder and also Tristan's."

For some reason I'd stopped watching what Jim was

doing as he prepared the picnic for us. I was watching his face.

His eyes.

And something wasn't right.

"Poor Tristan," he said, picking up an apple and cutting it in half in his hand with a large Chef knife—certainly a bigger knife than was needed for the job I've have thought. "He was really so clueless, you know?"

I nodded, watching his face and then the knife in his hands. My body had tensed and I could feel my heartbeat racing for some reason.

"I mean, you could just see what a mess he was," Jim said. "Ever see him drink a beer? He sips it like a little bird afraid it'll be snatched from him any minute."

And there it was.

How did Jim know how Tristan drank beer? How did he know unless he'd watched him do it? Tristan was poor. The only time he drank beer was when the older man came to see him in *Mégisseries*.

The older man who shouldn't be there. Nicole had slipped up. She'd said too much and when I began to ask questions she tried to make the save by lying and implying the older man was Matteo. But it wasn't.

It was Jim.

I felt a dizziness swipe across my brain and my knees went weak.

"Jules? You okay?"

"Yes, of course," I said too brightly.

Now what do I do? Should I ask him about paying for sex or spending time with the village juvenile delinquent?

My skin began to crawl and I rubbed the sensation away.

"Are you cold? I have an extra blanket."

"No, I'm good."

I stood up. I don't know why I did it. Sometimes my body knows more about what's going on than my head does. I had no concrete reason to fear Jim, other than the sneaking suspicion that he was some kind of sexual deviant. Okay, I guess that's pretty concrete.

"Where are you going?"

"No place."

"Then why are you standing?"

He got to his feet too and that's when I knew the pretenses were about to fall away. He knew I wanted to run. His body was tense and poised to reach out and grab me should I try.

"What's going on, Jim?" I asked softly, hoping to see the old Jim, the Jim I knew, take over.

"You tell me, Jules," he said, his eyes hooded and blank. I have never seen the person who appeared behind Jim's eyes.

The monster who appeared.

31

ALL HANDS TO THE PUMP

"If you run, I'll catch you," the monster said, his eyes watching me, his lips turned up in a malicious smile. Enjoying this.

"Why would I run?" I asked, my heart pounding in my chest until I thought I couldn't breathe. It was not yet totally dark but it would be in a few minutes. There was a bit of a moon.

But not enough light to run through the woods and not impale myself on a dead tree or trip over a fallen log.

I needed to think.

"You're looking toward the woods," Jim said easily. "That's not a good plan. I've got fox traps set up everywhere in there. Just one will snap your foot off at the ankle."

I tried to slow the pounding of the adrenaline into my bloodstream. I needed to pace myself. I was going to need every ounce of strength.

"I don't understand what's happening," I said, glancing down at the picnic.

He snorted. "Yeah, you pretty much ruined that, didn't

you? I don't even want to tell you what I spent putting this evening together."

The words stuck in my throat. My first inclination was to apologize. But I couldn't do it to the monster who stared impassively at me.

An image of Jim walking over to me from Madame Zabala's booth came to me. At the time I had been focused on the little white bag in his hand with our éclair in it. I should have been focused on his face. If I had I'm pretty sure I would have seen the same face I was looking at right now.

"Why did you kill Chevalier?" I blurted out.

"Bravo, Jules," Jim said, still not moving from his poised stance—ready to grab me any second. "Did you just work it out?"

"What possible reason did you have for killing him?"

"None. I'd never laid eyes on the guy before he came to Chabanel."

"Then why?"

"No reason." Jim grinned and spread his hands as a magician might. "What do you think about that? Here you and DeBray are falling over yourselves trying to find a motive and there never was one."

"I don't understand." I felt my adrenalin spiking and my heartbeat thundering in my ears. He was confessing. I was in the middle of the woods, at night, with a murderer. And not just any murderer. But one who killed for no reason, no provocation.

"It didn't matter to me *who* ate the poisoned éclair," he said with a shrug. "I chose the éclair as my instrument of death, if you will, as a symbolic gesture because you'd essentially ignored me for the two weeks prior to the fair while you and *les soeurs* baked night and day."

My stomach began to lurch uncomfortably as he spoke and I realized the man I'd been spending so much intimate time with these last several weeks was a sociopath.

"And planting the foxglove in Madame Cazaly's booth?"

"An extra bit of fun since the bitch always made it so obvious how disappointed she was that I wasn't Luc. Someone who, by the way, is being made a total fool of through all this. You do see that, don't you, Jules? The man's a complete bungler. Does he have a single suspect who isn't a joke? Oh, that's right, you've handed him the lezbos." Jim threw back his head and laughed. "Good one."

"What about Tristan?"

"Are you asking if I killed him? What do you think?"

"You knew him from *Mégisseries*, didn't you?"

"Very good, Nancy Drew. Done your research I see. Tristan was thinking of talking to you about all that—only, that's right, you don't speak the language, do you?"

"Talking to me about what?"

"About the fact that he was the one who tried to burn down *La Fleurette*."

"I already knew that. It's why he was in jail."

"Yeah, but I was the one who paid him to do it."

My stomach buckled again and I prayed I wouldn't end up vomiting on the ground.

Jim had spent that evening with me at *La Fleurette*. And all along he knew that Tristan was out there somewhere ready to torch it.

"*La Fleurette*," Jim sneered. "The so-generous gift from the amazing Luc. Destroying that dump was on my to-do list from the moment you moved into it."

I was working hard to control my fear which wanted to overwhelm me. My impulse was to go screaming toward the woods—to hide, to climb a tree. But if I let my emotions rule my next movements, I'd die.

Pure and simple.

"You don't think I didn't know you really wanted Luc? Do you have any respect for me at all?"

"Then why did you continue to date me?"

"At first I thought I could change your mind. And then it occurred to me that I could show Luc and everyone else how effing brilliant I was *and* get rid of one noxious bitch at the same time. After Madame C, I'd have gone after Madame B next of course."

"But if nobody knew you were the killer, how would they know how brilliant you were?"

Jim let out a sigh. "That's always the problem. In order to get credit, you have to implicate yourself." As he spoke he reached down and picked up my wine glass.

"There...there have been others?"

He pulled a small packet from his pocket and sprinkled its contents into my wine.

"Not in Chabanel. I did more than my share in Aix and a couple in Marseilles. This was the first time I did it on my home ground."

"You can't imagine I will voluntarily drink that," I said, hating the sound of my voice shaking.

"Oh, you'd be surprised what I can imagine. Anybody know we're out here?"

"Yes, lots. The Madame twins and Katrine."

"Oh, well. I guess I'll have to kill them all."

I saw the moment when he was going to take the step in my direction. I hated that I'd let him choose the moment but I'd been too paralyzed with shock to move.

One step closer to me was a split second less time for me

to live. I grabbed the wine glass out of his hand, sloshing the liquid down my hand. I pivoted to dart away but my shoes slipped on the wet grass.

His hand clamped down hard on my arm.

32

RIVER DEEP, MOUNTAIN HIGH

Luc stood on the front step of *La Fleurette*. It had been six weeks since he'd been here last. That was at the end of summer. Now he could see his breath in the evening air.

Madame Cazaly opened the door. She was dressed in her robe held tightly to her throat.

"Thank God you have come," she said, reaching out to him.

Confused, Luc stepped into the living room. The dog Cocoa raced to him and jumped up on his knees. Madame Becque emerged from the kitchen. She too was in her robe.

"How did you know?" she asked, her eyes darting from Luc to her sister.

"Know what?" Luc said. "Has something happened?" He glanced at the stairs and wondered why Jules hadn't come down.

"Madame Zabala is gone!" Madame C said, her face pinched with worry. "I came down to make a cup of cocoa and saw her room was empty."

"Gone?" Luc frowned. "Where would she go?"

"We don't know!" Madame Cazaly wailed. "You must find her!"

"Where is Jules?"

Luc's mind began to race. Had they sent Jules into town to get him? That would explain why she wasn't here now.

"Jules is with Monsieur Anderson," Madame Becque said.

"I see."

"You must find Madame Zabala!" Madame Becque said urgently. "She is sad, Luc. She...she is..." She looked at her sister whose face crumpled into a mask of misery.

"She may hurt herself," Madame C said. "We believe she may hurt herself."

"Over the loss of her grandson?" Luc said. He walked to the back of the house, wondering which direction the old woman might have gone.

"No, but it doesn't matter," Madame C said. "She is gone and we feel sure she means to harm herself."

Luc pushed thoughts of Jules and Anderson out of his mind. He had questions to ask Jules about Enora Roche and Marie Fournier but those could wait.

Finding Madame Zabala could not.

He turned to Madame C. "We'll find her," he said. "Tell me when you noticed she was not in the house."

∼

"You bitch! Now I'll have to do things a little differently." He clasped me in a bear hug, my back to his chest. His breathing was heavy and rasping in my ear.

I fought the feeling of futility from being trapped in his arms; my feet didn't touch the ground as he carried me back to the picnic blanket. Terror ratcheted up into my throat and I lashed out with my free hand.

The one still holding the wine glass.

I smashed it hard across his temple.

Jim screamed and released me and I fell forward onto the picnic, scattering dishes and wine bottles as I landed on my hands and knees. I grabbed one of the wine bottles as I lurched to my feet and turned to see him—clutching his face with a stream of blood trickling between his fingers.

I didn't stop him. I just made him mad.

"Things'll go worse for you now, bitch," Jim sputtered, wiping his hand on his slacks.

"How are you going to explain all the blood, Jim?" I taunted. "Got an answer for that? Luc knows where I am!"

"No he doesn't. He's not coming."

I needed to get past him to the line of trees. There was nowhere to run behind me. He was standing between me and safety. I hefted the heavy wine bottle in my hands. No way could I swing it at his face. I was too slow. He'd take the bottle away from me easily.

And beat me to death with it.

But I might be able to do something else.

"I'll give you a head start," I said. "Leave now. They might never find you."

"I'm not leaving. I'm killing you. Tonight. Right after we have our special picnic."

Okay, so if I thought he was insane before, I could see now that he'd invented a whole new level of crazy.

I forced my shoulders to slump forward, the wine bottle hanging limply from my fingers.

"Please don't do this, Jim," I said. "Please."

He wiped his face of the blood that continued to flow and took a tentative step in my direction.

I have to look resigned to this, I told myself. I can't look like I'm planning anything. Jim would be able to see it from a mile off.

I needed him to come closer.

Even though every step he took toward me made me want to curl up and die or run in the opposite direction, I had to let him come.

"You know I'm going to make it hurt," Jim said as he reached me, his hand grasping my chin, digging his nails into my flesh and shaking my face. "You know that, right?"

I drew back my arm with the bottle in it—visions of my high school soft ball pitching days zooming across my memory field—and slammed the bottle straight between his legs.

His eyes had been on mine so I saw the moment they glazed over and then rolled up into his head. He released my face.

I dropped the wine bottle and ran.

As I dodged the first fallen log before reaching the tree line, I could hear his howl of pain and rage but it was faint and far away.

By the time I hit the trees, all the light sucked out of my world. The sounds of Jim's howls should have been growing fainter.

But they weren't.

They were growing louder.

He was coming.

And gaining fast.

33

PAYING THE PIPER

Madame Zabala had not gone far.

But very nearly too far.

Luc brought Cocoa with him and while it was too dark to track the elderly woman with his eyes, both *les soeurs* seemed to think she would have gone back to her old house.

It was the house she'd lived in during the war. It was a falling down shack not a mile outside Chabanel. Luc was sure it was full of snakes and rats. But that wasn't what worried him.

It was perched on the edge of a small gorge.

If someone were intent on killing themselves, they could do no better than walking off the cliff into the void.

Luc didn't know how much of a head start Madame Zabala had on him but he knew that even a minute was long enough to prove fatal. He jogged, using his flashlight to keep him from tripping on the dark path. Cocoa ran ahead of him. Luc was grateful she didn't bark.

Anything might set Madame Zabala off.

He reached her house, a forlorn, dilapidated structure,

and saw the ghost of a dirt road that had once been the front drive. Without stopping, Cocoa veered around the side of the house and disappeared behind it.

Luc followed, his heart in his throat. The moment he cleared the side of the house he saw a shadowy figure standing silhouetted on the lip of the gorge. The only sounds were the ones made by his shoes as he crunched across sticks and dried leaves to where Madame Zabala stood, her back to him. Cocoa sat a few feet away. The dog whined softly.

"Madame Zabala," Luc called softly. "Please don't do this."

She turned to glance at him. She held a cane in one hand. She lifted it and pointed it at him until Luc realized she was telling him he could come no closer than the length of the walking stick.

"Leave me," she said.

"I can't do that."

"I don't want you to see this."

"Then don't make me witness it. Come away from the edge."

"No. I am tired."

"Then come back to *La Fleurette*. Come back to bed."

"I cannot rest."

"Then talk to me."

"You would condemn me."

"I would never."

"You don't know my crime."

"Tell me."

He saw her shoulders slump and estimated the time it would take to lunge at her, bat the stick away and pull her from the edge. He was still waiting for his moment when she looked past him, her face stricken, and dropped the stick to her side.

"Finally we will all have peace," she said as she stepped backward off the ledge.

∽

The day's sun hadn't reached the woods' interior. The ground was still muddy and sloppy from the recent rain. Up until now I'd been too stoked on adrenalin to feel the colder temperature. But as I slowed down to maneuver around the stumps and fallen logs, I felt it bore mercilessly into me.

As furious as he was, Jim had been smart enough to grab a flashlight before he took off after me. I looked behind me and saw the beam crisscrossing the woods between us as he raked it back and forth.

It was only a matter of time.

I'd already slipped twice in the muddy surface, once all the way to my knees, and I didn't know these woods. Not like the ones behind *La Fleurette*.

And Jim had said he'd booby-trapped them.

"Gotcha, bitch!" Jim crowed triumphantly.

I didn't turn to register the fact. I dove into a thick line of undergrowth, feeling every cut and tear as I did. Maybe he didn't see where I'd gone. Maybe he just saw me disappear. But once he got here—if I stayed put—he would quickly find me. I was frozen with indecision.

Do I keep trying to run through the woods? Do I hide and pray his flashlight beam doesn't hit me?

I heard him lumbering nearby and I pulled back into the thickest part of the bush I was sitting in. He was only about ten feet away. If I moved, he'd see me. If I didn't, with the next sweep of his flashlight, he'd find me.

I felt a wave of despair and I knew I didn't have time. If I didn't escape him, I'd die here tonight in these French woods. And maybe he'd be true to his word and come back and kill the Madame Twins and even Katrine.

Nobody suspected him. He wasn't on anyone's radar. If I died here tonight, more people would die in Chabanel.

I can't die.

My paralysis made my decision for me. I held my breath to be as still as I possibly could be. And I prayed.

There's something about serial killers—they seem to have a second or third sense. They know when to stop and when not to. They're not like the rest of us.

I'll never know why Jim chose that spot to stop and look around. I could see him standing there, just a shadowy figure with a flashlight. He was thinking, I could almost smell his brain cells burning. He reached down and rubbed himself where I'd slammed the wine bottle into him. And then he began doing a slow sweep of the bushes.

He knew I was there.

Dear God, somehow he knew it.

The second the beam lit up the bush I was sitting in I knew I didn't have the strength to climb out and run.

I'd been praying for a miracle and I know I'd made the cardinal mistake of not trying to make that miracle happen for myself.

I'd just sat there and hoped and waited.

I heard his crow of triumph and then the feel of his hands—iron-like and cruel—on my shoulders as he wrenched me out of the bush. I felt the branches rip at my clothes, my flesh. And my terror at knowing what was coming left me weak and gasping as he threw me onto the ground before him.

I thought he would say something to me—jeer, brag, something.

But the next thing I was aware of was an explosion of pain to my right side and midriff where he kicked me hard while I lay on the ground. Stars detonated in my brain and an icepick of cold agony reverberated through my solar plexus. Once the pain began to recede in vibrating waves, each a little less horrible than the last, I became aware again of the terrible cold.

I clawed at the dirt beneath me, my face close to his foot. His shoes looked so perfectly normal. I imagined what they would have looked like in a store window or maybe he bought them online months ago before the EMP.

Months ago when I was still in Atlanta and had every expectation to live past my twenty-seventh birthday.

When I moved I could feel that something was broken. I felt crooked, like I couldn't straighten up, let alone stand.

It didn't matter. Jim reached down and grabbed me by the scruff of my jacket and began to drag me. I screamed in pain. It was my arm. It hung useless by my side and I had to fight to get to my feet. Jim paused long enough to allow me to and when I was finally standing, I stumbled along beside him, his hand on my collar and wrapped up tight in my long hair.

The pain in my arm was like nothing I'd ever experienced before. I prayed to go into shock. I'm not sure I didn't pray for death.

Jim was talking as we walked but I either didn't understand—there could be something wrong with my ears—or he was talking gibberish. Where he was leading me wasn't far and I was grateful when we came to what looked like a clearing with one side devoid of trees.

At first glance I thought it was a pasture. Or maybe a roadway.

He dragged me closer and I saw why there were no trees. It was a cliff.

We stood at the edge, his hand tightly ensnared in my hair. The half moon illuminated the rocky crooks and crannies in the drop off. It started off gently, with a few saplings growing sidewise out of the granite. And then it fell straight down.

Even the moonlight was no help in seeing how far down it went.

Jim held his flashlight out over the cliff.

"Listen to this," he said. For a moment he sounded like the old Jim. Like he was telling me about something interesting he'd heard in the village. I heard the faint sound of a waterfall in the distance. Then he opened his hand and let the flashlight drop.

I listened. And waited. I didn't hear it hit.

So this is how he was going to play things, I thought.

A night time rendezvous turned tragic when the impetuous American Jules accidentally fell off a cliff.

Knowing his plan seemed to help wake me up.

Not that my arm was any less broken. Not that I had any weapons or tricks up my sleeve.

But at least I was alert enough to go down fighting.

And go down I did.

I swiveled on one foot and smashed my head into Jim's chin, putting everything I had into it.

I had the brief satisfaction of hearing his *ooff* of surprise before his hands hit my chest hard and I felt myself falling backward off the edge.

34

NEVER IN A MILLION

I hit the slope on my back and slid faster and faster, head first, down the cliff front, my one good arm windmilling frantically to catch something, anything that might stop my fall.

A tree sapling scraped me and I lashed out and grabbed a branch. It slipped through my fingers—slick with sweat and blood. I slammed into the next one—bushy with dried leaves and I latched onto a small slim branch. My grip held.

As soon as I stopped sliding, the sound around me came back at top volume. My shoulders were off the cliff, my hips resting on the last part of the slanting ledge, a fistful of young tree in my hand.

The roots of the tree started to give.

"Son of a bitch!" Jim swore from up top. "Dear God why do you have to make everything so hard?"

I couldn't get my breath. My chest felt crushed with terror and the inability to take a breath. My arm began to spasm.

There was no way I could hold on. All he had to do was wait and I'd eventually have to let go.

A part of me actually longed to let go.

Suddenly Jim appeared. His face angry and terrified all at once as he careened past me, arms flailing, with a scream I will hear to the day I die as he fell all the way to the bottom of the gorge.

My hand holding the tree began to shake violently. The sight of Jim's face—so close and so full of terror at what was happening to him—was imprinted in my mind. I couldn't shake the image. Or process what had happened.

Why did he do that? Did he hate me so much he would throw himself off a cliff to get at me?

I wanted to close my eyes and end this horror. Once and for all. I looked up to the half moon and I don't know what I intended, whether to pray or say goodbye but all of a sudden rocks and dirt rained down on my upturned face and I twisted my head away to avoid it.

When I did, I screamed at the pain that shot up my bad arm—and without meaning to—released my grip on the tree branch.

I slid quickly, my shoulder and hips suddenly free of contact with the rock as I started my final fall before I felt strong hands grasping my jacket and jerking me to a stop, prompting another strangled screech of pain from me.

My heart was pounding with the pain and with the knowledge of how close I'd just come to toppling down the cliff after Jim.

"I am sorry to be hurting you," Matteo said, panting heavily as he slid down next to me and immediately began fitting me with a rope harness.

I groaned. *So clearly I have died after all*, I thought.

"You may let go now, Madame," Matteo said as he snapped a tether into the gear loop and jerked it taut. The agony in my arm had subsided to a dull roar and I hoped that shock had finally set in to numb the pain. My mouth was dry and I saw sparks igniting in my field of vision.

Crap. I was passing out.

Some part of me felt Matteo's hands on me, patting my face, his breath on my cheeks. I felt the hard metal rim of the canteen mouth on my lips, the smell of the stale water startling my senses. The water was wonderful but also awful. I tried to open my eyes but I felt I was floating and under the circumstances I thought it was best to keep it that way.

You know how those near death experiences where the patient says he could see himself rise up above his body and look down? Well, it wasn't exactly like that but close. I could smell and hear and taste but it all felt like it was happening to someone else. I was so grateful for the pain in my arm to be gone that I didn't care about anything else but I was conscious enough to know that if I saw a light I shouldn't go toward it.

Matteo wrapped his jacket around me and the contraption of webbed harnesses he'd attached to me and then used a carabiner to attach a rope that he'd secured from up top. As he cinched it tight he inched his way back up the cliff with me strapped close beside him—laboriously, slowly—until we reached the top.

He carried me to a tree and began unbuckling all the straps and bindings he'd attached to me. He had a radio which he spoke into in rapid incomprehensible French and then he turned to me and began gently to inspect me for injuries.

"How did you know I was here?" I gasped, utterly amazed that he was here. Amazed that I was alive. And that Jim was...gone.

"Madame Becque told me where to find you. Plus you

have a stridently piercing scream. I easily heard it through my back fillings."

I groaned as he touched my bad arm. He quickly began to fashion a splint for it.

"But *why* did you come?" I asked, gulping past the waves of pain. "How did you know to come?"

"An informant revealed to the police this evening that a crime had been committed by Monsieur Anderson. I came here to detain him."

"Well, mission accomplished, Detective Matteo," I said with a shaky smile as I closed my eyes. "I'd say you detained the crap out of him."

My eyes fluttered open and I'll be a son of a gun if I hadn't made the bastard smile. That's okay. He deserved to feel good about what he'd done tonight. In fact, I'd have to say Detective Adrien Matteo was my hero. Ooops, maybe saying that was a bad idea. Now I wanted to throw up a little.

"Can you see him?" I asked. There was no way I could turn my head to look down or get near enough to the edge to look down. It would be a miracle if Jim was alive. But still. It was *Jim*. We'd been friends.

"You do not need to worry about him any more."

"You need to get an ambulance for him."

"One thing at a time."

I can't tell you how sensible I thought that sounded. In fact, even without drugs, Adrien Matteo was slowly morphing into one of the most intelligent people I'd ever met. Honestly, I think I loved him.

I shook my head at the thought and that hurt. A lot. So I closed my eyes and just let him do everything.

I figured it wasn't totally out of the realm of possibility that Matteo might be right about many things but at least one thing for sure: one thing at a time.

35

SHINE ON

Two weeks later

Some might call it stubborn to sit outside in early November. In fact I know a few people who call it exactly that but it doesn't stop at least one of them from sitting with me out on the back terrace—the fire pit blazing—and both of us hunched in our heavy winter coats.

Well, actually my coat isn't actually *my* coat. How could it be? When I packed to come to the south of France six months ago I had no idea I'd need a winter coat at some point in my long tenure here. So I was snuggled deep inside one of Madame Cazaly's wool overcoats, a mug of mulled wine in my hands and the village head cop next to me to remind me with nearly every utterance how I need to be careful about mixing alcohol with pain meds.

Because make no mistake, when the police car finally came to drive me and Matteo to the hospital in Aix I was in need of some serious pain meds.

But as I sat here on the terrace now, two weeks later, my arm in a cast and a sling, my pain meds carefully measured out by those two psychos inside—three if you count Madame Zabala who looked very much like she'd moved in with us for good—my hot wine in hand—*and oh, did I mention the part about the police chief at my side?* a warm glow suffused through me that had very little to do with the fire pit or the mulled wine.

"So tell me again how you saved Madame Zabala from doing a header off the *petite gorge*," I said. I knew this was somewhat of a sore subject with Luc since while *he* was saving a ninety-year-old from jumping off a cliff which would certainly have demanded the reflexes of oh, a somnolent koala bear, *I* was fighting for my life against a wily, serial-killing psychopath on the other side of the very same gorge.

Not that Luc would've blown off saving Madame Zabala to come rescue me if he'd known about it, but it's nice thinking he might.

"You have heard the story many times," Luc said dryly.

He was quite enjoying being back in my good graces—if that's really where he was. Honestly, what with all the excitement I hadn't given it a whole lot of thought.

Ha. If you believe that!

"I want to hear the part about how Madame Cazaly followed you and was standing behind you when Madame Zabala made her grand gesture."

"As you know," Luc said patiently, drinking his wine, "as soon as I snagged Madame Zabala and pulled her to safety she fell into Madame Cazaly's arms and the two wept and apologized and buried the axe."

"Very good idiom use," I said. "But it's a hatchet."

"It makes no sense, whatever it is."

"And tell me again where I was when all this heartwarming crap was going on?"

"I think you were hanging by a vine over an eighty-foot gorge. But not to worry. Matteo was on his way."

"If I'd known he was coming I would have let go."

Luc made a tsking sound. "Now, Jules, that's not very nice. Matteo saved your life and there's no other way to look at it."

"I know, I know. And I'm grateful."

"You don't sound grateful."

"Well, I am. And the Madame Twins have been baking him *tarte tropézienne* for the past three days."

"He and all of us at the station are very thankful."

"Seriously, though. I know Matteo saved my life. I just can't get over that he had to. I can't get over that I didn't see through Jim."

"None of us did. He'd been living in Chabanel for four years."

"Killing people throughout the countryside."

Jim broke his back and both legs but enough saplings had slowed his descent such that he miraculously survived his fall. Since airlifting was a thing of the past, he was taken by an ancient and extremely bumpy ambulance to Aix where he was treated and then driven to Lyons where he would stand trial.

That was an unfortunate turn of phrase because poor Jim would never stand in the real sense ever again.

It seemed that Enora Roche and Marie Fournier—in a burst of confessional angst—had gone to the police station to tell Luc that Anderson had attempted to blackmail them about the murder. When Luc wasn't available, they unloaded to Matteo who promptly arrested them but also lit out to find Jim Anderson, stopping first at Anderson's house. When he found that empty, he went on to *La Fleurette* where Madame Becque was only too happy—in an attempt to sabotage my romantic picnic, no doubt— to tell him exactly where Jim and I were.

"So what was the deal with Enora and Marie Fournier?" I asked.

"Anderson saw them together and made them believe his testimony of their conspiracy would shoot them to the top of the suspect's list in Chevalier's murder."

I had to admit I'd had the same thought about them when I saw them together, which is why I'd gone to Luc to accuse both of them of Chevalier's murder.

A fact that Luc very gallantly didn't bring up now.

"Back in school," Luc continued, "they'd been lovers but their careers and other people had served to separate them for several years. When they found themselves together again, their mutual hatred for Lucien reminded them of how much they loved each other and they reconnected."

"Oh my gosh I've got a tear in my eye. Right there. See it? That is so sweet."

"Sarcasm does not suit you, *chérie*. It makes even the most beautiful women harsh."

"So Jim saw them together and then what? Because I talked to Eloise and she said it sounded like Enora and Marie were going to find him and kick his ass."

"I must have a word with Sergeant Basile. She is much too free with her mouth. In any case it seems Anderson saw Madame Roche and Madame Fournier share a kiss in an alley. When Enora approached him later to try to explain, he said he liked the idea of the two of them paying for this murder more than poor Madame C."

"He was playing God," I said. "Choosing who would go down for the crime *he* committed."

"Initially he framed Madame C for Chevalier's murder because...well, his reasons are immaterial at this point," Luc said.

But I knew why he'd done it because Jim had told me why. It was because Madame C had made clear that she preferred Luc to him for my affections.

"Enora Roche said she offered Jim money not to say anything but he just laughed. While they were of course innocent of Lucien's murder they were concerned that circumstantial evidence—backed by such a credible testimony from Anderson—would send them both to the gallows. They thought killing—or rather *confronting*—Anderson was their only chance to live unbothered."

"Whoa. Do you know for a fact that they intended to kill him?"

"I do not. And since in the end they opted to come to the police instead of go out and find Anderson that fateful day, we don't need to go there, do we? Do you like that? It's another idiom, I believe."

"It's slang."

"Really? Are you sure?" He frowned. "What is the difference?"

"You are the strangest kind of cop I ever heard of."

"I'll take that as a compliment."

I shivered under the coat and drained my wine cup.

"You are cold, *chérie*?"

It was nice that he called me *chérie* but I couldn't help flashing back to the last time someone had asked me that same question. I still hadn't totally assimilated how I felt about the fact that I'd so totally and badly misjudged Jim. I never even had a clue.

A Bad Éclair Day

And somehow, after all the drama and the moments of me being just so glad to be alive and Luc using that as an excuse to hug me or kiss my forehead from time to time, he'd taken to coming back to *La Fleurette* each evening.

I'm sure the Madame Twins Plus One were doing their bit to invite him, so delighted were they that he was back in the picture. But also, I looked forward to his visits.

I'd missed him.

And that was all very well but there was still the matter of the issue that had driven us apart in the first place. And if you know me at all, you know I won't let a little happiness, mulled wine and moonlight keep me from getting to the bottom of that—no matter how miserable it makes me in the long run.

Amazingly, Luc turned to me as if he'd read my mind and said, "I am sorry for blocking your trip back to America two months ago."

I sat up straight and instantly felt an ugly ripple in my broken arm and took a deep breath to fight the pain until it subsided. I can't tell you how delighted I was that Luc was finally admitting he was wrong. Maybe we really were going to get back on track.

"And so you'll step back now," I said, "and not interfere if an opportunity like that comes up again?"

He didn't speak and I didn't know what to make of that. Was he apologizing or wasn't he?

"The twins seem to think you're in love with me or something," I said.

"I would prevent you from leaving even if that were not the case."

"So you *are* in love with me."

"Is there more wine?"

"Look, Luc, the fact is I can't leave regardless of how

many boats show up at my door heading back to America. I can't leave *les soeurs*. But I can't handle not going because *you're* stonewalling me. You see that, right?"

"Then what does it matter that I am stonewalling you?" Luc said with a frown, "if you won't go back regardless?"

"It matters because it has to be *my* decision. Surely you can see that? I mean I know we're sitting in a house dating back to the twelfth century but lights or no lights, it's still 2017."

"As long as you do not try to leave," Luc said, "I am happy for you to think it is your decision."

"Oh. My. God. You are seriously trashing this beautiful moment between us! How can you—the most close-mouthed person in the universe—*not* be able to keep your mouth shut *now* of all times?"

Luc leaned over and claimed my mouth with his own. It was swift and unexpected and I instantly felt the heat shoot through me. I moaned and he pulled back.

"Your arm?" he murmured, his eyes full of concern.

I shook my head, my lips just inches from his.

I have to say, whether it was the pain meds or the relentlessly romantic Provençal moon, I found myself overwhelmed by the feeling—impossible to believe in any sane world—that being stranded in a foreign country in a post-apocalyptic world…had never felt more right.

"So now what?" Luc said.

I put my good hand on his cheek. It was rough and solid. Not unlike Luc himself.

"*Now*," I said, "I think we get this party started."

Be sure and check out *Croak Monsieur!*, the next book in the *Stranded in Provence Mysteries!*

WHAT'S NEXT

To see what happens next to Jules in post-apocalyptic Provence, be sure and check out Croak, Monsieur!, Book 5 of *the Stranded in Provence Mysteries*.

Here are the first three chapters.

I
Like Falling Off a Log

I'm pretty sure the horse was on to me.

It stood there in the farmer's pasture looking at me through half-lidded eyes, with a very definite *oh-hell-no-you're-not-climbing-on top-of-m*e vibe going on.

You see I have a singular instinct about animals. I can read their most obvious intentions. Like when a dog is snarling and straining at the end of his chain in an effort to try to reach me? I'm pretty sure teeth will be involved if I don't keep out of his reach. Or a goose that races up to me, hissing? *Not* wanting to be petted right now. Learned that one the hard way, I have to say.

My name is Jules Hooker and I have recently been

forced to learn all manner of things the hard way since coming to the south of France eighteen months ago for an extended stay. And by *extended* I mean *permanent* since the day after I arrived a dirty bomb exploded over the Mediterranean prompting an electromagnetic pulse which ended all twenty-first century conveniences and communications across Europe and the United Kingdom.

That's right. No TV, no telephones, no trains, no cars. Oh, hell. I'm getting depressed just thinking about it.

Any way, the point I'm laboring to make is that as a result of said catastrophe I am now standing in the French countryside on a beautiful spring day attempting to cajole a horse into letting me ride him so I don't have to wear out my shoes walking everywhere.

"You are sure you have ridden before?" said the horse's owner, a corpulent farmer in his fifties. He frowned as he watched me regard the horse.

I snorted and waved my hand nonchalantly at the man.

I was determined that nothing was going to sour this deal for me. I don't care if this horse goes by the well-earned name of *Diablo* and is single-handedly responsible for creating paraplegics up and down the French coast, he's going to be my new mode of transportation from here on out.

"Me ride good," I said in my fractured French. My language skills had actually gotten much better in the last several months but since they were nonexistent when I first came to this country, that's not saying a whole lot.

The farmer shrugged and pulled down the stirrups that had been threaded up into the saddle.

I wiped my slightly dampened palms against my jeans and approached the horse. He'd stopped looking at me—

the horse that is—which made it easier for me to pretend I wasn't more than a little nervous about all this.

I grabbed the reins in my left hand, and put my right hand on the back of the saddle.

"Bend your leg," the farmer said gruffly.

I did and he boosted me up and into the saddle. As soon as I settled into place I felt better and the spasmodic butterflies that had started to gather in my stomach began to dissipate. The fact is I really do know how to ride. I'd ridden most of my girlhood at various stables all over Atlanta and the north Georgia mountains. I even rode in hunter-jumper competitions during high school, which actually was the root of my problem now.

A routine fall in the ring during a lesson when I was eighteen resulted in a broken arm and prevented me from getting right back up on the horse as everyone knows you're supposed to do. Eight weeks later, by the time my arm was out of a sling, I'd developed a healthy irrational fear of riding.

And since the state of Georgia had repealed that state law demanding all horse-mad teens ride under any circumstance, I did what any sane person would do when faced with a brand new fear: I quit.

But right now I was sitting in the saddle and took a deep breath and tried to let my body's memory take over. I closed my eyes to feel the sun on my face and felt the horse's muscles quivering between my legs. The horse—*Roulette*—stood perfectly still which I was grateful for.

"*Bon*," the farmer said, clapping his hands in satisfaction. At the sudden sound both horse and rider shied violently.

The horse went one way and unfortunately I was not lucky enough to go the other. The second I felt the animal jerk underneath me I squeezed with my legs in a desperate bid not to fall off—which just served to urge him faster into his frenzied bolt.

Needless to say my eyes were wide open now.

"Hold on!" the farmer yelled needlessly.

Visions of me wrapping my arms around the animal's neck flooded my brain but I was too terrified to unclench from the handfuls of mane I was clutching. I felt the horse's muscles gather beneath me in a knot of energy. I didn't know this farmer's pasture or the parameters of his land. I didn't know where the field began or ended, whether there were water hazards or potholes, rings of fire or quicksand. And I'm pretty sure old *Roulette* here wasn't thinking of any of those things either.

As I watched the ground rush by beneath me, I thought of bailing out but the memory of my fall so many years ago came back to me. I couldn't afford to break my arm—or worse. Not now when life was so hard just doing basic things. I had to somehow stay on.

Not that far ahead I saw what looked like a stone wall. From this distance I couldn't tell how high it was.

Fortunately that problem was resolving itself by the second since *Roulette* appeared to be intent on heading directly for it.

Did the horse jump? Would he slam on the brakes right before the wall, sending me flying over it? My fingers gripped for whatever bit of reins were flapping loose by his neck. In order to turn the horse—which would also slow him—I'd need to let loose of his mane. I couldn't do both—hold onto the mane and steer him with the reins. And yet I could not let go of the mane. I just couldn't.

I watched the wall come closer and closer and felt the familiar sensations of hyperventilation sweep over me.

My natural instinct was to lean forward—back to my impulse to wrap my arms around his neck—but I knew I really needed to do the opposite of that. Sitting bolt upright would help slow him. It went against the raging fear that was now had me in its grip but the sight of the quickly advancing wall—now clearly way too high to jump—made me force my shoulders back and drill my seat bones down hard into the saddle.

I felt him slow down. Just a bit.

The wall was still approaching but he was no longer wildly galloping toward it. Encouraged, I unclenched one hand from his mane and grabbed for the flapping rein.

The wall was flying toward me now. I either had to make up my mind to jump it—*Dear God, don't let that be what happens*—or somehow direct his head *away* from it. I pulled on the reins and saw one of his ears flick back at me as if he might listen to me.

I pulled harder and he turned his head, slowing just a little. His body followed. Now we were racing alongside the stonewall. But there was still the problem of potholes. Most farm pastures do not resemble a polo field. It would be easy for an out-of-control horse to turn an ankle in a hidden divot, thereby catapulting me into the world of broken backs and colostomy bags. (I could only imagine what might pass for one in post-apocalyptic France.)

I continued to pull on the rein until the horse was finally heading back in the direction we came. Out of the corner of my eye I could see the farmer standing where we'd left him. As soon as I had the horse's head pointed toward the farmer, Roulette slowed way down. It wasn't a trot but it was at least manageable. I unclenched my other hand from his mane and now had both hands on the reins. As soon as I did, he dropped dejectedly down into a bone-rattling trot and I realized somewhere along the way I'd lost a stirrup.

I didn't bother trying to find the stirrup. My only goal at this point was to get off him without breaking anything vital. Like my neck.

"How was the test drive?" the horrible farmer called out as we trotted up to him.

I had no breath to answer him. My hands were shaking on the reins and I was pretty sure my legs would not hold me up when I finally dismounted. As it happened, I didn't have to worry about that.

Someone in the gravel driveway of the farmer's house slammed his car door just as *Roulette* came to a halt. Instantly, the animal shied again, swiveling out from underneath me and shooting away. In my mind I will always see the action as something out of a cartoon where Wyle E coyote remains suspended in air for a few painful seconds before slamming to the ground.

Basically, one minute I was about to swing my leg off to dismount and the next minute I was face down in the grass—all air having been smashed out of me with what felt like a baseball bat.

When I could breathe again, I peeled open my eyes to see that Luc DeBray was squatting next to me—grinning in his most annoying—although admittedly terribly sexy—way. Before he'd even helped me to a sitting position and began inspecting my limbs for any breakage, I realized it was likely *his* car door that had spooked *Roulette* the second time. So yeah, I was glad to see Luc all laughing it up at a situation that *he'd* caused.

"I thought you said you could ride," the farmer said.

"Tell him," I wheezed to Luc, still fighting for air, "that if he doesn't give me the damn horse, he doesn't get *les soeurs'* pies."

The two ninety-plus year old sisters whom I live with are renowned throughout Provence for their *tartes aux mirabelles*. They'd struck the deal with Monsieur Obnoxious here to let us have the temporary ownership of the horse for a weekly delivery of two pies. I know it seems odd that I'd still want the damn horse after it tried to kill me *twice* but you seriously have no idea how far two miles is on foot unless you've hoofed it a few times a week loaded down with groceries.

Luc laughed, his hand resting on my shoulder. Seriously sexy and pretty much officially my boyfriend for the last month, Luc DeBray was also the chief of police of Chabanel the village where I now live. It's the reason he actually has a car door to slam in order to be able to spook my horse. Except for my friend Thibault, Luc is the only one for a hundred miles who owns a car.

"Are you sure, *chérie*?" Luc asked, his golden brown eyes molten as he regarded me.

Like a lot of people I've met over here, Luc thinks I'm basically helpless if not downright self-destructive. He's madly chauvinistic. I think I missed the worst part of that sort of thing in my generation back in the States but I have to say, in little doses it's kind of sexy and fun.

Trust me, Luc goes way past *little doses* on an hourly basis.

"Yes, I'm sure," I said. "As long as you don't sneak up behind me in your car when I'm on him and honk the horn I should be fine. Tell the farmer we have a deal or no pies."

As Luc helped me to my feet and told the farmer that all systems were still go, I was relieved to realize that last night's rain had softened the ground enough such that the fall hadn't been all that bad. I'd be bruised tomorrow but most of that was on my hips so wouldn't show. Unfortunately my favorite denim crop pants looked to be a total loss.

"How did you know I was here?" I asked as I walked with him back to his car after making arrangements with the farmer to come out and take possession of *Roulette* tomorrow. But of course I knew the sisters would have told him.

"You are limping, Jules," he said, frowning at me.

"I'm fine," I said. "You still coming for dinner tonight?"

"Don't I every night?"

Just before I got to his car I turned to get one last look at the demon on wheels who'd just tossed me in the dirt and who was now mine-all-mine. The farmer was leading him back to the barn. Roulette's head was down and I could see grass sticking out of his bit. He seemed to have calmed down pretty quickly from the whole door-slamming trauma. I was glad.

One way or the other, I was determined that he and I were going to make this work.

Even if it killed me.

2

Touch and Go

That evening the starry starry sky was nearly obliterated by the leafy branches of the plane trees that crowded our back garden. I walked out onto the back terrace, my dog Cocoa at my heels, a flute of Prosecco in one hand, and sent a silent prayer skyward that the rumor I'd heard in town today that electricity was coming back soon was true.

I had a fairly decent stack of firewood on the side of the house—covered with a moldy tarp against the rain— but I hadn't given up hope that the electric oven now sitting in the garden shed might one day be of use to us again.

Sometimes I amaze myself at how my life has changed since the EMP. If I thought two years ago that I'd think nothing of rummaging around the countryside for wood to burn in an oven so I could eat a stew with not even any meat in it, well, I'd never have believed it.

Luc was waiting for me by the outdoor fireplace.

"Dinner was great," he said as he shoved a piece of wood into the blackened maw of the fireplace.

"I hope you told the twins that," I said, although I knew he had. He always raved about their cooking which might be one reason why the old dears were so in love with him. In the last eighteen months, Luc and I had had a very bumpy start and during those times when we were not together, *les soeurs* had been very unhappy about it—and very vocal.

Luc leaned down to tussle Cocoa's ears. I don't think there's a time when I see him and the dog together that I don't remember the incident that brought her into my life—or how close I came to losing that life. I wonder if Luc ever thinks of that.

Knowing Luc, I'm sure he does.

Chauvinistic and fiercely protective—like a man who'd stepped right out of the nineteen fifties— Luc was like nobody I've ever met before. Certainly not back in the US. I'd often thought that the similarities between how we're all forced to live now—without the modern conveniences we'd become used to—and how my parents grew up in the fifties were striking.

Don't get me wrong. I love all the moments in front of the fire and the long walks and the real food and the things we have now as a result of no more cars or iPads, electric blankets or constant social media.

But I'd still kill for five minutes with the Internet.

"You are pensive tonight," Luc said, settling down on the outdoor settee. He held his arm out to indicate he was ready for me to cuddle up with him. Much to my amusement, Cocoa beat me to it and jumped up next to Luc and curled up by his hip.

I laughed and sat down on the other side of her, pleased that while disappointed, Luc didn't move her.

"I was just thinking about how much better my life will be with a horse in it," I said.

He frowned. "Are you sure? He looked dangerous to me."

"Everything looks dangerous to you," I teased. "As long as nobody shoots off a gun by his head while I'm on him, I'll be fine."

Clearly not convinced, Luc just smiled and shook his head.

"I heard a rumor that electricity is coming back to Chabanel," I said.

"Where did you hear that?"

"It's a rumor, Luc. The whole point of a rumor is that the source isn't reliable. So? Is it true?"

He lifted one shoulder—a very Gallic, very French gesture that I've seen him do only about a thousand times. It's amazing how much detailed articulation a French person can deliver without uttering a word. Which, considering my less-than-solid ability to understand the French language, is a good thing.

"*Peut-être*," he said. *Maybe.*

"So you know or you don't know?"

"There is no timeline for it."

"I won't hold you to an exact timeline. By the end of the year? By this time next year? By summer?"

"Not by summer I think."

I nodded. "So this time next year."

"And what will you do when you have electricity again? The laptops still won't work. The car engines have all been fried."

"They'll ship more cars in that haven't been fried," I said. "And the Apple store in Aix will start selling laptops again."

"Which you will pay for with what, may I ask? *Les soeurs'* pies?"

"Very funny."

But he did have a point. It was all very well and good to cobble together a life when everyone around you was doing the same thing but as soon as France got around to rebooting, I'd need to be ready.

Unspoken between me and Luc was the fact that when the electricity came back, so would my ability to go home. In fact, if a little podunk village like Chabanel was expecting electricity within the year, it meant that ships and airplanes would soon be running again to and from France.

I felt a splinter of excitement—triggered by the idea of going home—but dulled by the pain of saying goodbye to this man whom I had grown to care so much for.

Of course I would go home when I was able to. It never occurred to me that I wouldn't.

Did Luc think I'd stay?

Like so many things between us, it was a subject I didn't want to raise and I was pretty sure he wouldn't either.

The main schism between us had happened six months ago when an opportunity had come up for me to go back to the US and I found out that Luc had blocked it. Without asking me, without informing me. He'd just made it go away and hoped I'd never find out about it. But I did find out about it. Even now, with so much that had happened between us, and with the growing belief that I was sure as every day passed it was love, even now the fact that he'd done that and never admitted it had been wrong—even now I felt the sting of that betrayal like a tiny burning nugget of fury that threatened to reignite at any time.

Later that night after Luc left, I found the sisters in the main salon, the central fireplace blazing. While I was keenly aware that the old dears were almost always cold and I certainly didn't begrudge them a cozy fire in the evening after all their hard work, I was also sharply aware of all the hours of finding, splitting, and stacking firewood that their evening of pleasure would cost me in the days to come.

Mentally admonishing myself for my lack of charity, I joined them in the room. All three cats—Neige, Tiny Tim and Camille—were curled up by the hearth. Each one half feral, they watched me with hooded, untrusting eyes as I sat down. Did I mention I'm usually the one who feeds them every night? Ingrates.

"Chief DeBray has gone home?" Madame Becque asked, not looking up from her sewing.

"Yep," I said. "Off to keep Chabanel safe and sound for one more day."

Madame Cazaly—Madame Becque's sister—looked up from her knitting and smiled sweetly at me. She was as different from her twin as night was from day. Where Madame Becque was all hard edges and disapproving glances, Madame Cazaly was sweetness and light. I didn't have the full resume on how they'd come to be living together, but one had married and one hadn't. Madame C— the married one—was long widowed and both were veterans of the French Resistance during the last world war.

One thing the old girls did have in common was a determined reticence about something that had happened in the war. I knew it was something big and I knew it would take all my powers of deduction and manipulation to get it out of them. But I would. One day I would find out what their big secret was.

Meanwhile, when the lights went out all over Europe, the three of us had banded together and honestly it's been a pretty good arrangement. They're ancient, of course, so I'm their arms and legs. They generally order me about like one of Scarlett O'Hara's field hands but truthfully they work even harder themselves.

And they're both amazing cooks.

"You are okay, Jules?" Madame C asked, frowning. *Remember? She's the sweet one?*

Cocoa came and jumped on my lap, prompting hisses from two of the three cats even though she was nowhere near them. I tugged my fingers through the half-Labrador's fur on her head.

"Luc says we might get lights back by the end of the year," I said.

I noticed the twins exchange a look and as usual I had no idea what it might mean.

"We are happy without electricity, yes?" Madame C said lightly, focusing back on her knitting. The unsteady flicker of the single kerosene lamp that illuminated both their needlework reminded me that it was a miracle neither of them had gone blind trying to work.

"Personally I miss Netflix." When both sisters looked at me in confusion, I waved a hand at them. "Just kidding. But you seriously don't care if the lights don't come back on? Seriously?"

"What is it you think the electricity will give you, Jules?" Madame B said sharply. "Will Luc love you more? Will the *cassoulet* taste more flavorful? Will the grape harvest be sweeter?"

I didn't answer her because on the tip of my tongue—and I'm forever grateful that it stayed there—was the retort that the coming electricity would allow me to go home. I guess I didn't have to say it because both women looked at me with arched eyebrows as if daring me to say it out loud.

"You are happy here, are you not, Jules?" Madame C said. "With us?"

"Of course," I said with mounting frustration. "You know I am."

"And yet you wish to leave," Madame B said bitterly.

"America is my home! How would you feel if you were stranded far from Chabanel?"

"I would never leave Chabanel in the first place," Madame B said tartly, her insult to me loud and clear: *You left your home so it must not have meant that much to you.*

"People travel, Justine," I said, feeling my frustration mount and not sure if that wasn't because I knew that at least on some level she was right and I just hated to admit it. "People travel without it meaning they don't care about their homeland."

"*Si tu le dis,*" Madame B said with a shrug as if that ended the conversation. *Whatever you say.*

I clenched my jaw in frustration.

Is that what was wrong with me? Is my problem that I want to go home but I also don't want to leave the twins or Luc or the life I've created here? Is it because I know what I want is ultimately going to mess up everything I have?

I looked past the deep tufted arm chair toward the kitchen where *les soeurs* had made our dinner tonight. The floor is tile, the counter tops prehistoric stone and the refrigerator—which no longer works of course—is now used to store pantry items. My friend Thibault had built a large wood-fired oven for us shortly after we moved to *La Fleurette*. It's almost impossible to get it hot enough to actually bake anything and pure torture trying to maintain it at any kind of specific *degree* of heat.

And yet we eat well every night with time left over for sitting by the fire, reading, musing, talking.

It is a good life. I readily admit that. It's just not the one I planned or wanted.

"It doesn't matter," Madame B said as she stood up and eased the kinks out of her ninety-three year old back. "Jules can have everything in the world she thinks she wants and still she will look for more."

Don't you love it when people talk about you in the third person right in front of you?

"*Non*, Justine," Madame C said. "Jules will be as happy as she decides to be."

"You guys know I'm still here, right?" I said.

"*Un petit malin*," Madame B said, shaking her head as she picked up the kerosene lantern. *Smart ass.*

Madame C instantly started packing up her knitting and I watched with mounting horror as Madame B teetered toward the stairs, sloshing the liquid in the hurricane glass as she moved.

We'd already had one fire here at *La Fleurette* and while it's true the ancient *mas* was mostly stone, I wasn't in a hurry to see how much of it would burn the second time.

I stood up and took the lantern from her, waiting by the foot of the stairs to light the way upstairs to our bedrooms.

Have I mentioned how badly I want electricity to come back to my world? Can you imagine just twisting a little knob and *voila*! you get light?

Like magic!

If we get electricity again I swear I will never complain about another thing ever again.

3
All You Need is Love

Luc stood at the window of his office at the *Police Municipale* and looked out over the town square. The morning breeze shifted the dead leaves from the looming plane trees in a languid sweep down the village main street. He could see the town hall and the *Place de la Maire* from here. Since there was no more traffic to worry about it was always a very peaceful *tableau* these days. Now with the budding Madonna lilies and the ubiquitous array of bright red geraniums that every shopkeeper it seemed had set out against the backdrop of cobblestones, the picture was as about as charming and quaint as one could imagine.

"Did you sleep here, Chief?"

Luc half turned to see his sergeant Eloise Basile standing in the doorway, a cup of coffee in one hand and a flaky croissant in the other.

"No," he said slowly. "I'm just in early this morning."

"You mean on time."

"Do you need something, Sergeant?"

"Madame Gabin said you had a letter from the *Direction Centrale de la Sécurité Publique* you didn't pick up." Eloise pulled an envelope out from under her arm and waved it at him. "Says it's urgent."

Luc sighed. Communications had improved somewhat since the EMP had shaken the country eighteen months earlier but postal letters were still largely the main form of correspondence. And while the mail came on trucks not horse and wagon, it still took on average of three days each way for the trip from Paris.

He held out his hand and Eloise handed him the letter.

"Where did you get the croissant?" he asked as he glanced at the address on the letter. It was from Paris, just as Eloise had said. A fissure of anxiety flashed through him. While nine out of ten times correspondence from the General Directorate of the National Police was just announcing a new generally ridiculous rule that would make his job a hundred times harder, that tenth time was actually something that would make his job impossible.

He wondered which one this would be.

"Matteo brought them in," Eloise said, referring to Luc's second in command Adrien Mateo, a sour and officious little man with no sense of humor or soft edges to make him more palatable. Luc often wondered if he'd still keep Matteo on if he weren't so desperate under the present post-apocalyptic circumstances.

"Matteo?" Luc said in surprise as he pulled the single sheet of paper out of the envelope. "Really?"

"I know. Madame Gabin was in shock too. What is it, Chief? Are we all getting battery-operated mopeds?"

Luc scanned the sheet. It was a formal invitation for all the chief heads of the National Police throughout France to meet in Paris—tomorrow—for a two-day mandatory training conference. Luc read it twice to confirm no option for not attending. He sighed.

"Where is Matteo?" he asked.

"In his office, I think," Eloise said. "Is it bad, Chief? What does it say?"

Luc tossed the sheet on his desk.

"No, it's not bad. It means that Adrien will be in charge

for two days while I'm in Paris for an all-heads police conference. I'll need to leave immediately."

I'll need to get word to Jules that I won't be able to come tonight.

He glanced around the office. He already had several sets of clothing here in the office. He wouldn't need to stop at his apartment first.

Eloise picked up the sheet and read it. "He's not going to be happy about being in charge with no car," she said.

"Just tell him I want to see him," Luc said, running his hands through his hair.

"You know this is probably about the Marseille thing," Eloise said.

Luc stopped and looked at her. "What Marseille thing?"

"You know, about the upsurge in organized crime there. It was in the paper."

Did anyone still read the newspaper? They must or at least Eloise did.

"What did it say?"

"Just that the police force in Marseille is powerless to control the new crime wave. Nice is the same and I heard Lyon and Dijon were edging that way. I'll bet that's why they're calling you all together."

Luc snorted. If what Eloise said was true this trip to Paris officially sounded like a huge waste of time. What did it matter to Chabanel or any other small Provençal village if Marseille was crime-ridden?

Hadn't that always been the case?

"The paper said the murder rate in Marseille is triple what it used to be."

"Sounds like a good reason to stay away from Marseille. Put that down and go tell Matteo I need to see him."

Eloise placed the letter on his desk and hurried out of his office.

Luc sat down heavily in his chair. It was a long drive to Paris—at least seven hours even with no cars on the road any more. He'd hoped that the next time he'd visit Paris he'd have Jules with him. But this was not the time.

Thinking of Jules he felt a flash of discomfiture. While she'd said she'd forgiven him for blocking her chance to return to America on a tramp steamer last fall, he knew her feelings about it were still conflicted. And that was in large part because he hadn't been as contrite as the situation called for.

The fact was he wasn't sorry. Jules was a smart girl. She saw that.

She saw that while he was unhappy at how his thwarting her opportunity had caused a breach between the two of them, given the chance again he'd likely do the same thing again. He couldn't lie to her. What was the point of a relationship if he did that? He couldn't lie to her and he had not been able to promise her that he wouldn't do it again.

Not just in his role as Chief of Police of Chabanel but because of how he felt about her. The last thing he could do was allow Jules to get on an unsecured boat that was just as likely to take her to the slave markets of Dubai as Miami.

Jules didn't understand how dangerous it was. That was his job. Whether she liked it or not—or forgave him or not —he would do that job for her own good no matter how much of a bastard it made him look.

4
On the Road Again

The next morning, I awoke excited and ready to hop on

my bike and head back to Monsieur Dellaux's barn to take possession of *Roulette*. I was proud of the fact that I hadn't let yesterday's mishap in the pasture build up in my head to the point where I was afraid to get back on him.

That just shows how desperate I was to get some mobility that didn't include a bike or my own two feet. Even a horse who has shown every sign of wanting to kill me is better than walking.

I flung open the window of my bedroom where it looked out over the back garden. Spring was definitely doing its thing in the greenery department in the garden. The sisters had planted rows of tomatoes, corn, cabbages and sweet potatoes and as a result we pretty much never went without a salad or a hand-picked vegetable for any of our meals—amazingly even in winter because they canned so much last fall. Or rather they had *me* can so much last fall.

La Fleurette was the ancient *mas* that Luc had discovered last year as a vacant property and arranged that the twins and I could live in. As old as the hills—and I mean that nearly literally—it is entirely made of stone with a back garden that the sisters have transformed into our own private vegetable-producing Costco. Personally I know nothing about gardening—at least that was true a year ago. Since then, given all the time Madame C has me yanking weeds and tilling the rocky soil, I'm pretty sure I could do a master class in gardening for my own YouTube channel by now.

If YouTube still existed.

I dressed quickly and made it half way down the slick stone staircase to the main floor—lured by the aroma of coffee and *crêpes* wafting from the kitchen, when I could tell we had company. First Cocoa abandoned me at the top of the stairs with a sudden happy yip—letting me know the visitor was a friend—and secondly I heard the low murmur of my friend Thibault's purring bass.

I always jokingly say that Thibault is an acquired taste because with his long greasy hair and his big beefy shoulders squeezed into various leather jackets, he looks at first site like a deranged biker guy. But like most gentle giants he's a pussycat and I'm not sure what I would have done without him in Chabanel.

Plus did I mention he has a car?

"*Bonjour*, Jules!" he called out as I joined him in the big cavernous kitchen where *les soeurs* were in the process of feeding him everything that wasn't moving in the kitchen.

We air kissed and I settled down at the table next to him. Normally I wouldn't act as if the sisters were there to wait on me but the kitchen was their domain and they didn't typically like me rattling around in it when I could be doing something else—like weeding the garden, running errands for them, or scouring out the fireplace.

Today it looked like they were going to let me eat breakfast with Thibault without having to work for it first.

"*Bonjour*, Thibault," I said, nodding my thanks to Madame C as she poured me a cup of coffee from the large French press the sisters kept on the stove. The stovetop was made hot with just a few sticks of kindling. It was the oven that required half my day to find and continually apply fuel to keep it burning long enough to roast or bake something.

"What brings you to *La Fleurette* at this hour?" I asked, blowing on my hot coffee.

"Besides *les soeurs' crêpes mirabelles*?" he said with a grin, revealing an impressive array of jam chunks in his straggly beard. "I have news."

I glanced at the twins who must not have been that impressed with whatever news he had since they were pretty much doing what they normally do every morning after they finish making breakfast—prepping for lunch.

"Oh, yeah?" I said, feeding a corner of a *crêpe* to Cocoa. "What kind of news?"

"You can leave immediately," Madame Becque said as she scanned the kitchen to see if there was anything else to do or anyone else to order about.

"Leave?" I said, feeling a chunk of ice begin to form in my stomach. "Who leave? Where? Why?"

"*You* leave, *chérie*," Madame C said happily. "With Monsieur Theroux. To Marseille."

I snapped my head back to look at Thibault. "Marseille?"

His mouth full of *crêpes* and jam, Thibault nodded. "*Oui*," he said in a muffled voice. "We can pick up Diego on the way."

"Whoa, whoa," I said, turning to address Madame B since as usual she was the one who would determine who did what and when. "I can't go anywhere today. I'm supposed to take possession of the horse today. Remember? The pies? The deal you made with Monsieur Dellaux?"

Madame B snorted. "Monsieur Dellaux has his tarts. He can hold the horse for one more day."

I threw up my hands in a dramatic expression I knew the old girls would appreciate—for all the good it would do me.

"But I want to get back up on the horse," I blurted. And it was right then I realized the only reason I hadn't let yesterday's equine setback get to me was because I knew I was going to go back today. But if I didn't go back? All I'd be left with was the impression that I couldn't ride that horse.

Worse, that's the impression the horse would be left with too.

No, it couldn't wait. Not again. I had to get back there and get back up on him.

"You can ride the horse any time, *chérie*," Madame C

said, admonishingly. "We need you to go to Marseille today with Thibault."

"You will spend the night," Madame B said.

There was no sense in arguing and I knew I might as well come to grips with that right now. I was going to Marseille. Today.

I pushed my coffee mug away petulantly and felt the combined prongs of disappointment and annoyance needle into me.

"Can I at least ask *why* I have to go to Marseille today?" I asked peevishly.

"I have found a very good buyer for *les soeurs'* blackberry wine," Thibault said. "He is interested in several bottles—possibly a case a week—and will pay much more than the Chabanel market."

I sighed. Our *cave* at *La Fleurette* was lined with the blackberry wine the twins had spent most of the winter bottling. At the rate we were selling them at the village market, the whole batch would go bad before we could earn back the time and money that had gone into them. So yeah, I could see how what Thibault had discovered in Marseille was good for us.

"How did you find this guy?" I asked, not really caring. Because Thibault was one of the few people in all of Provence still with a vehicle, he got around a lot. It wasn't surprising he'd have a contact in Marseille.

"I met him through someone else," he said enigmatically. Thibault was involved in a lot of different businesses —most of which weren't legal *before* the apocalypse. I decided not to press the point.

"We are packing lunch and dinner," Madame C said. "You are not to eat in Marseille. It is much too expensive and you have no money and nothing to trade."

Thibault snorted out a laugh and I gave him a baleful look.

"What about dinner tonight? Luc will be coming as usual."

"Chief DeBray has sent a message," Madame C said. "He is off to Paris for the next two days. He will not even know you are gone."

"Fine," I said, standing up to go to the French doors to let Cocoa out into the back garden. "Whatever."

"You will enjoy it, Jules," Thibault said as he stood up, dropping a few pounds of *crêpes* crumbs from his lap to the floor. "Marseille is *magnifique*. And on a beautiful spring day *comme aujourd'hui*? Wait until you see the harbor. Your eyes will pop out of your head."

Once I'd started to accept that I wasn't going riding today, I began to mull over what I might wear to a seaside town. I had a sundress that I'd traded a week's worth of surveillance on the shopkeeper's husband last fall—have I mentioned yet I'm the village private detective?—and I hadn't had a chance to wear it yet. It wasn't Prada but it looked great on me. I was only sorry Luc wouldn't be there to see me in it. Thinking of Luc made me think of something else I'd heard about Marseille which suddenly crawled to the forefront of my thoughts.

"Isn't Marseille supposed to be dangerous?" I said. "I thought it was supposed to be the most crime-infested city in all of France or something?"

All three of them laughed and generally hooted down my comment.

"It is perfectly safe if you stay in the right areas," Thibault said.

"You have a bodyguard the size of an ox!" Madame B

said, somehow managing to insult both me and Thibault in one go, which I have to say was not a first for her.

"You will be fine, *chérie*," Madame C said, amusement dancing in her eyes.

I sighed in resignation.

I could only hope that the next time I met *Roulette*, he'd wouldn't take my no-show as a sign of weakness.

5
Beautiful Disaster

Marguerite emerged from the back seat of the Peugeot 508, sliding across the leather upholstery and feeling her Valentino silk rockstud dress ride up her thighs. Her driver and bodyguard had long since stopped opening the door for her and when Marguerite had complained to her husband about it, he told her she should be glad he let her ride in the limo at all. Very few in Marseille still drove.

A part of Marguerite thought the apocalypse actually had drawn a much darker line between the haves and the have-nots. Before then, it wasn't always possible to look into the eyes of a woman wearing Prada or Manolos and see her worth. She could just as easily be a shop girl careful to spend her few extra dollars on quality accessories.

But now it was different. Now the wealthy had the luxuries as usual and the middle-class had what the poor used to get by with. And as for the poor? Marguerite straightened her shoulders as she stood on the sidewalk and looked down the street. A line of cafés straight ahead reminded her that the best part of Marseille—the street life—would never change. And rich or poor, all could enjoy.

She teetered down the sidewalk on her five-inch heels and glanced in the shop windows as she walked. To be sure there were fewer and fewer decent stores. And certainly nothing like Cannes or Paris. Somehow even without lights or petrol, shipping transport or transatlantic communications, fine jewelry was still being bought, *haute couture* was still being shown and worn, and the very best life had to offer was still being lived by those who could afford it.

Not in Marseille, of course, she thought as she caught a glimpse in one of the shop windows of her bodyguard, Titouan. Like most single-minded thugs, he rarely got distracted from his job. He watched her and constantly scanned the environment for threats.

What must it be like not to have a life of the mind? she wondered. No interior life at all? She watched Titouan scrutinize the sidewalk, the empty street and the cafés before them and she could see his mind—like a machine—assessing threat probabilities, checking and re-checking hazards.

She was glad of course that he was good at his job. Tito would protect her. He would die for her. He just wouldn't obey her. A schism of frustration pierced her and she saw her face harden in the reflecting shop windows.

At least Tito was her father's man, not Fabrice's.

If it had been up to Fabrice, Marguerite would go out into the world alone and unprotected. In no way would he ever consider spending the money on a bodyguard and driver for her. Even so, it didn't stop Fabrice from ordering Tito about as if he were his own private man servant. And Tito, like the good automaton he was, took it all unflinchingly and without emotion.

She stood in front of a *brasserie* to examine the menu. There were very few occupied tables inside. Not many people could afford to eat out these days. Not many restaurants could afford to stay in business. She turned away.

No, Tito would be no help to her. He would obey her father's orders—and even Fabrice's. But not hers.

Because just like Tito, she thought with a familiar hopelessness, she was owned lock, stock and Gucci pump by the men in her life with the money.

***

Fabrice watched the boy approach. He was dressed simply, his jeans clean, his t-shirt frayed but unsoiled.

He thinks this is a job interview, Fabrice thought humorlessly as he watched the young man approach. He crossed his arms and cocked his head as he observed the boy. *He walks as if he has never been to a sea harbor before.*

Perhaps that was true. With the recent cessation of all shipping or cargo transport, only pleasure boats frequented the harbor these days.

And a poor boy from the slums of Marseille would know little about that.

"Monsieur Charlevoix?" the young man said, hurrying his pace as he recognized Fabrice waiting for him.

Fabrice put his hands on his hips. Normally he would wait until the other man held out a hand to shake before ignoring the hand. But Fabrice had something else in mind today.

"You are Monsieur Alaoui?" Fabrice asked, showing his teeth in an approximation of a smile.

"Yes! Marco," the boy said.

As Marco neared, Fabrice saw that the young man was very attractive. A well-formed, athletic body, cheekbones that hinted of a distant Arabian bloodline perhaps, and full lips with dark eyes. Yes, he was very good looking.

"Well, Marco," Fabrice said. "Walk with me and let us talk, eh?"

"Yes, Monsieur Charlevoix."

Marco put his arms behind his back and held his elbows like an awkward schoolboy. His lashes were long and thick and framed guileless eyes.

Is it really possible for anyone to be this innocent?

"My man Titouan may have told you a little something about the job," Fabrice said as they walked down the dock. Two fifty-foot yachts were on opposite sides of a narrow wooden dock that jutted out from the boardwalk. "It is not skilled work but then you are not skilled, are you?"

"No, Monsieur. But Tito has told me a little."

Fabrice narrowed his eyes at him. "And how do you know Titouan?"

Marco grinned. "I didn't until a few days ago," he said. "We met at a bar and got to talking."

"Have you ever worked as a deckhand before?"

"No, Monsieur."

"It is not difficult work. You can follow orders, can you not?"

"Yes Monsieur."

"Very good. We sail from Marseille at least twice a month. My wife hates it, of course. She would much rather be in Paris or on the Côte d'Azur."

"Yes sir."

"You are not to speak to my wife, Marco. Do you understand?"

"Of course, Monsieur."

"And I will not pay you until after your first sail and then only if I am satisfied with your performance."

"Okay."

"You don't sound sure."

"Oh, yes, Monsieur! I am very sure." Marco's eyes glittered with excitement and strayed to glance at one of the yachts.

"Would you like to see where you will be working?" Fabrice said, taking a step in the direction of the Anna Marie on his immediate left.

"Yes, Monsieur," Marco said eagerly. "I would like that very much."

I'll just bet you would, Fabrice thought, a thin smile on his lips and his heart hardening into a sliver of ice in his chest as they walked.

***

Padre limped across the deck of the forty-five foot sloop. He'd made it a point to be on board today hours before he needed to be. In fact he didn't really need to be here at all. The vessel virtually sailed itself, it handled so easily. But its owner, his employer, didn't know that. And even if he had, he still would not have been able to get the boat out of the harbor on his own.

Padre sank onto the padded leather bench on the bridge, his knee aching as he did. He felt the cigarettes in his pocket and counted them with his fingers. Six left. He hadn't had the money to buy more before boarding. Tito didn't smoke but perhaps the new deck hand Monsieur Charlevoix was planning to hire today did.

Bile churned in Padre's stomach as he thought of his employer. He'd worked for Charlevoix for nearly a year now. The job was easy enough—sail out to the Gulf of Lions while Tito prepared lunch for the Charlevoixes and then return—all the while posing in his ridiculous captain's costume and directing Charlevoix's men to manage the sails.

They were shorthanded today. But the loss of their most recent deck hand was not unusual.

Few self-respecting young men would put up with the abuse for long.

Padre looked down at his soiled trousers and a shimmer of malicious satisfaction pierced him at the thought of how Charlevoix would react when he saw him. But what could the *putain* do about it? Not sail?

Up until this morning, a part of Padre's job had always been wearing the expensive captain's uniform. The pin-corded trousers with the razor creased pleats, the ridiculous hat, the cartoonish jacket with the gaudy fringed epaulets. Padre was literally being paid to stand at attention in a circus costume and sail the yacht up and down the harbor while Monsieur and Madame Charlevoix sunned and ate and fought.

In truth, Charlevoix spent most of his time below deck which was a relief to everyone—particularly Madame Charlevoix.

But today would be different. Today was Padre's last sail with the Charlevoixes.

After last week's sail Charlevoix had fired the deck hand —in truth the man was an idiot but what did Charlevoix expect from the pool he chose his candidates from? Luis or whatever his name was had been drunk from the start of the sail and only got worse as the day went on. When Charlevoix fired him, Luis was too stupefied to even know he'd lost his job.

For some reason Charlevoix believed Luis's bad behavior was Padre's fault. That was typical of Charlevoix because he needed to blame someone for every unfortunate thing that happened to him. He told Padre that he didn't owe him his day wage for the outing due to the fact that

Monsieur had been seasick and felt a non-nauseating joy ride was the least of what Padre was being paid to provide.

So he didn't pay him. Even now Padre found it hard to believe. The week in between sails had been a difficult one. Unable to pay his rent, Padre lost his apartment. Desperate for a place to sleep, he'd sold the captain's hat for two nights in a flop house, where he was certain he'd picked up bed lice. Then, last night in an attempt to steal a packet of cigarettes, Padre had been chased and beaten by the proprietor of the *tabac* near his former flat.

In his attempt to flee, Padre had fallen on the cobblestones—slippery from fish heads and sewage—and twisted his knee. Even now it throbbed. The *tabac* owner had blackened Padre's eye and stripped him of his captain's jacket.

Today, dressed as the bum he had finally become, Padre had decided he would finally and with great satisfaction show the *putain* Charlevoix what a stomach-churning sailing trip was *really* like.

To continue reading, check out *Croak, Monsieur!, Book 5 of the Stranded in Provence Mysteries*.

ABOUT THE AUTHOR

USA TODAY Bestselling Author Susan Kiernan-Lewis is the author of *The Maggie Newberry Mysteries*, the post-apocalyptic thriller series *The Irish End Games, The Mia Kazmaroff Mysteries, The Stranded in Provence Mysteries, The Claire Baskerville Mysteries,* and *The Savannah Time Travel Mysteries.*

Visit www.susankiernanlewis.com or follow Author Susan Kiernan-Lewis on Facebook.

Made in the USA
Columbia, SC
27 June 2025